Classics of Modern Science Fiction

SHADOWS IN THE SUN

9

Books by Chad Oliver

NOVELS

Mists of Dawn (1952)
Shadows in the Sun (1954; new edition 1985)*
The Winds of Time (1957)
Unearthly Neighbors (1960; revised 1984)*
The Wolf Is My Brother (1967)
The Shores of Another Sea (1971)*
Giants in the Dust (1976)

COLLECTED STORIES

Another Kind (1955)
The Edge of Forever (1971)

NONFICTION

*Ecology and Cultural Continuity As Contributing Factors In
the Social Organization of the Plains Indians* (1962)
*The Discovery of Humanity: An Introduction to
Anthropology* (1981)

*Classics of Modern Science Fiction

Classics of Modern Science Fiction

SHADOWS
IN THE SUN

CHAD OLIVER

Volume 9

Introduction by George Zebrowski
Foreword by Isaac Asimov

Series Editor: George Zebrowski

Crown Publishers, Inc.
New York

Published by Crown Publishers, Inc., One Park Avenue, New York, New York 10016 and simultaneously in Canada by General Publishing Company Limited

Manufactured in the United States of America

CROWN is a trademark of Crown Publishers, Inc.

Library of Congress Cataloging in Publication Data
Oliver, Chad, 1928—
    Shadows in the sun.
    (Classics of modern science fiction ; v. 9)
    I. Title.   II. Series.
PS3561.L458S49   1985   813'.54   85-3768
ISBN 0-517-55867-X
10 9 8 7 6 5 4 3 2 1
First Edition

*To Dad and Mom
The two finest shadows
Under one of the better suns*

Retrieving the Lost

by Isaac Asimov

T HE HISTORY OF contemporary science fiction begins with the spring of 1926, when the first magazine ever to be devoted entirely to science fiction made its appearance. For a quarter-century thereafter science fiction continued to appear in magazines—and only in magazines.

They were wonderful days for those of us who lived through them, but there was a flaw. Magazines are, by their very nature, ephemeral. They are in the newsstands a month or two and are gone. A very few readers may save their issues, but they are fragile and do not stand much handling.

Beginning in 1950, science fiction in book form began to make its appearance, and some of the books retrieved the magazine short stories and serials in the form of collections, anthologies, and novels. As time went on, however, it became clear that the vast majority of science-fiction books were in paperback form, and these, too, were ephemeral. Their stay on the newsstands is not entirely calendar-bound, and they can withstand a bit more handling than periodicals can—but paperbacks tend to be, like magazines, throwaway items.

That leaves the hardback book, which finds its way into

public libraries as well as private homes, and which is durable. Even there, we have deficiencies. The relatively few science-fiction books which appear in hardback usually appear in small printings and few, if any, reprintings. Out-of-print is the usual fate, and often a not very long delayed one, at that.

Some science-fiction books have endured, remaining available in hardcover form for years, even decades, and appearing in repeated paperback reincarnations. We all know which these are because, by enduring, they have come to be read by millions, including you and me.

It is, of course, easy to argue that the test of time and popularity has succeeded in separating the gold from the dross and that we have with us all the science-fiction books that have deserved to endure.

That, however, is too easy a dismissal. It is an interesting and convenient theory, but the world of human affairs is far too complex to fit into theories, especially convenient ones. It sometimes takes time to recognize quality, and the time required is sometimes longer than the visible existence of a particular book. That the quality of a book is not recognizable at once need not be a sign of deficiency, but rather a sign of subtlety. It is not being particularly paradoxical to point out that a book may be, in some cases, too good to be immediately popular. And then, thanks to the mechanics of literary ephemerality, realization of the fact may come too late.

Or must it?

Suppose there are dedicated and thoughtful writers and scholars like George Zebrowski and Martin H. Greenberg, who have been reading science fiction intensively, and with educated taste, for decades. And suppose there is a publisher such as Crown Publishers, Inc., which is interested in providıng a second chance for quality science fiction which was undervalued the first time around.

In that case we end up with Crown's *Classics of Modern Science Fiction* in which the lost is retrieved, the unjustly forgotten is remembered, and the undervalued is resurrected. And you are holding a sample in your hand.

Naturally, the revival of these classics will benefit the publisher, the editors, and the writers, but that is almost by the way. The real beneficiaries will be the readers, among whom the older are likely to taste again delicacies they had all but forgotten, while the younger will encounter delights of whose existence they were unaware.

Read—

And enjoy.

Introduction

George Zebrowski

SHADOWS IN THE SUN (1954) was Chad Oliver's second published novel, and still his confessed favorite. The Ballantine Books edition appeared in simultaneous hardcover and paperback, and was followed by British, French, German, and Italian editions published between 1955 and 1967. The second American edition came out in 1968, in the Ballantine Bal-Hi books paperback series for students, featuring a special two-page introduction to parents and teachers about the novel's theme and a reading level indicator at the back of the book. Neither of these aids was very enlightening. This Crown edition is the novel's first American edition in nearly two decades.

The novel was well received. "The theme is an alien masquerade on Earth," wrote Damon Knight in the May 1955 *Science Fiction Quarterly*; "the treatment is original and compelling." J. Francis McComas, the great co-founding editor of *The Magazine of Fantasy and Science Fiction*, wrote in the *New York Times Book Review* for December 5, 1954:

With this, his first adult book, Chad Oliver, author of a number of excellent short stories and a first-rate juvenile, has written what is very likely the best science fiction novel of the year. In a quiet, realistic, entertaining story, he has brought one of the great science fictional themes down to earth. For, in this book, the almost insoluble problem of the Terran man versus the superman from outer space is worked out . . . within the confines of one small American town . . . to the men of other star systems, Terran man may be nothing more or less than a savage. And what happens to the savage when he meets civilization head-on? What happened to the savages of our own world when their lands were colonized by the culturally superior white man? In essence, then, the problem posed by this novel is the salvation of the savage. And while the whole equation is not worked out—no earthly anthropologist is yet wise enough to do that— enough of the solution is intimated to make this one of the most thought-provoking pieces of fiction, scientific or otherwise, this reviewer has read in years.

One of Oliver's wry solutions to the problem of the earthborn savage is to let us live in "reservations" known as cities, where we can be contained and managed by the aliens, who will control the liberated countryside. Another solution is to let us destroy ourselves. Alien control will simply follow our natures, since we exhibit both the tendency to crowd into cities and to threaten our survival through warfare. The aliens would go unnoticed.

Writing in *The Magazine of Fantasy and Science Fiction* for April 1955, Anthony Boucher, the other editor and co-founder of that once-great publication, announced that *Shadows in the Sun* . . .

clearly establishes Chad Oliver as one of the leading young talents in the field. . . .Oliver is a trained professional anthropologist as well as a skilled writer; and he uses his knowledge of anthropological field techniques to revitalize completely the familiar theme of "There-Are-Alien-Observers-Among-Us." I can't think of anyone who has more sensibly and convincingly portrayed members of a highly advanced civilization who are *not* supermen, or who has treated more logically and humanly the problems of one of us in adjusting to such a culture.

P. Schuyler Miller, writing in *Astounding Science Fiction* (May 1955), stated that the novel showed "Chad Oliver's study of anthropology sinking into his thinking and writing, and I'm inclined to say that it's the best science fiction with an anthropological theme that I have seen." He also underscored one of the book's key ideas: that humanoid intelligence may be common in the galaxy, and that the greatest differences between its civilizations may be cultural, not physical. Oliver at one point in the novel does permit the existence of wholly alien Others, "intellects vast and cool and unsympathetic," in H. G. Well's famous phrase, but he is not concerned with them in this book except as a future problem. The problem for Paul Ellery, anthropologist, is to decide whether he wants to be educated to take his place in the alien society. This possibility holds a great attraction for a scientific worker; so much will be revealed to him. His other choice is to remain with his own kind and help its development as best he can.

In my introduction to *The Shores of Another Sea*, another Oliver novel in this series, I mentioned Kingsley Amis's disappointing view of *Shadows in the Sun* (in *New Maps of*

Hell, a study of science fiction published in 1960). He is clearly blind to the novel's anthropological materials, focusing instead on irrelevancies. Paul Ellery is, for Amis, an unlikely anthropologist: six feet tall, two hundred pounds, and an American from Texas, of all places. I noted that this was in fact a fair physical description of Chad Oliver himself. Amis goes on to discuss certain features of genre fiction. These features are, of course, completely overcome by the novel's scientific authenticity, and if Amis had known any anthropology he would have seen how misplaced his remarks were. I bring up these failures to show the impotence of purely literary or formal critiques of genuinely scientific science fiction. The similarities in Oliver's novel to conventional genre narrative strategies are superficial; the differences are profound.

Amis's lapses into literary and cultural parochialism seem strange in a critic who professes to understand science fiction, especially when discussing a novel of first contact with an alien civilization. But his reaction may also explain why too few readers appreciated Oliver's work in the 1950s; they failed to notice the subtle use of anthropological concerns in his stories and novels. This was not the case, happily, among the better critics and reviewers; Amis seemed to have been the most noteworthy exception.

An interesting professional notice for *Shadows in the Sun* appeared in a 1955 issue of the *American Anthropologist*. Evon Z. Vogt of Harvard University wrote:

> The publication of this delightful book calls the attention of social scientists to Chad Oliver (a graduate student of anthropology at UCLA) as a first-rate science fiction writer. The plot is similar to Huxley's *Brave New World*

but with an interesting extension in scope. Instead of dealing merely with Earth, Oliver brings "civilized" man in from other Earth-type planets. The "savages" are not American Indians but ourselves. This startling discovery is made by Paul Ellery, Ph.D. in Anthropology, who is making an anthropological study of Jefferson Springs, Texas. Throughout the book, effective use is made of the concepts and data of contemporary anthropological writers. Anthropology definitely comes of age in science fiction in this unusual book. . . .

This description of Oliver's novel shows how far removed it is from routine genre efforts involving aliens and flying saucers.

Thirty years after its first publication, *Shadows in the Sun* has lost nothing of its reputation—yet the last edition was published in 1968! Readers who now take anthropology for granted in the works of Ursula K. Le Guin and Michael Bishop have responded with interest to the new Crown editions of *Unearthly Neighbors* and *The Shores of Another Sea*. A major article on Chad Oliver by L. David Allen appears in Everett F. Bleiler's *Science Fiction Writers: Critical Studies of the Major Authors from the Early Nineteenth Century to the Present Day* (Scribner, 1982), in which only seventy-five authors are covered. Oliver is ranked in the top ten percent of science fiction writers. Four of Oliver's books are listed in Neil Barron's flawed but influential *Anatomy of Wonder* (1976, second edition 1981), in the annotated bibliography of the modern period (1938–1975). The annotations in this work are too often inadequate, but the core bibliographies, however incomplete, are valuable tools. Further proof of Oliver's continuing modernity comes from Harlan Ellison, who wrote the following when he heard that a new edition of *Shadows in the Sun* was being planned: "I have been an enthusiastic admirer of *Shadows in the Sun* since it was originally published. Among other virtues, it was one of the first genuine New Wave novels, and that long before there was a New Wave. Chad Oliver is among the most underrated writers in science fiction."

The New Wave appellation has some plausibility, in my view, because of Oliver's focus on character and place. The novel has a here-and-now reality and the emotional undercurrents that show up in all of Oliver's fiction. The science is quite real, however, and so the novel might be claimed for the "hard science fiction school" as well, except that this description is still incorrectly applied to science fiction based on physics, astronomy, chemistry, and even biology. But Oliver, as a scientist, did bring his professional sensibility into his fiction (and he is comparable to scientist-authors Arthur C. Clarke, Gregory Benford, Isaac Asimov, and others); and this combination of science and human character, expressed in a graceful, literate style, was one of the professed ideals of the science fiction New Wave of the 1960s, however often that movement rode off in other directions. The challenge of combining the writerly virtues with those of science fiction is still with us.

One example of how Oliver met this challenge, as both a writer and anthropologist, and as a science fiction writer, is made clear when Paul Ellery decides to stay on Earth rather than be educated by the aliens. He stays *because it would be bad anthropology for him to go*; he would be exchanging one set of cultural problems for another, for ones that he would have to learn from scratch. In formal terms, character, plot, science all move dramatically forward at the same time, subtly, with feeling and poetry, streaming implied ideas left and right from the main action. Compare this with Richard Dreyfuss donning a red suit and rushing to board a flying saucer in the film *Close Encounters* (a work that has more than a few echoes of Oliver's work in it, but none of his sophistication).

The final, moving validity of Paul Ellery's decision to stay on Earth in order to delve more deeply into himself and his kind, reveals a profound anthropological commitment, one that I suspect is much like Oliver's dedication to his own work as a scientist and teacher. Suddenly we see that cultures are angular views of the universe, and that their unique physical and cultural perspectives are to be treasured; each is a response to the mystery of existence. Paul Ellery chooses his humanity, knowing that progress cannot be imported; to be real, it must be won from within, in endless ways, just as understanding must be built up afresh in each individual.

1

A T FIRST IT had been plain stubbornness, disguised as scientific curiosity, that had kept Paul Ellery going. It was different now.

He *had* to know.

He sat at the corner table of the Jefferson Springs Cafe, alone as he had always been alone in Jefferson Springs. There wasn't much to look at in the small dining room—a grimy electric clock that had been exactly six minutes slow for the past two months, a somewhat battered jukebox, with tired technicolored bubbles, dying on its feet, the inevitable painting of Judge Roy Bean's *Law West of the Pecos*, a greenish-glass case filled with warm candy bars. Paul Ellery looked anyway, with restrained desperation. Then he pushed back his plate with its remnants of chicken-fried steak and French-fries, and began to draw wet circles on the varnished table with the bottom of his beer bottle.

There was a boxlike air-conditioner stuck in one window, consisting of a fan that blew wet air into the room. Ellery could hear the water from the fan hose dripping down to the ground on the other side of the wall; and inside the cafe it was so humid that even the wood was sweating.

Except for the hum and drip of the air-conditioner, there wasn't a sound. It was like sitting in a cave, miles beneath the earth.

Waiting for an earthquake.

Ellery tried to ignore the unwanted little animal that kept shivering up and down his spine on multiple ice-sheathed feet. He tried to remind himself that the animal was imaginary. He tried to tell himself that he had nothing to fear. He tried to look calmer than he felt.

It was incredible.

The month was August, the day was Thursday. He was in Jefferson Springs, a town of six thousand inhabitants, in the state of Texas, a part, usually, of the United States of America. It was eight o'clock in the evening and it was hot. Some one hundred and twenty miles to the north was the city of San Antonio, where the Alamo had given way to the Air Force. Sixty miles to the south was Eagle Pass, and on across the river was Piedras Negras, in Mexico. Everything seemed perfectly ordinary. Indeed, Jefferson Springs could hardly have been a more average town if it had tried.

On the surface, there was no cause for alarm.

He finished his beer, and it was as hot and sticky as the rest of the cafe. He briefly considered ordering another one, but abandoned the idea. Instead, with great deliberation, he dug his pipe out of his back pocket, where he carried it like a .45, and filled it with tobacco from a cloudy plastic pouch. He lit it with a wood stick match, broke the match, and dropped it artistically into the beer bottle. Then he aimed a wobbly smoke ring in the general direction of Judge Roy Bean and watched it battle the current from the air-conditioner.

"The hell with all of you," he said, silently but inclusively.

He was the only customer in the Jefferson Springs Cafe. He had been the only customer, so far as he could tell, for the past sixty-one days. Cozy.

The first week he had been in Jefferson Springs he had played the jukebox religiously. It had seemed like sound field technique, and it had helped to fill up the emptiness with a semblance of life. As he was somewhat selective in his choice of popular music, however, this hadn't proved precisely a sedative to his nerves. The jukebox in the cafe was typical of those in small Texas towns. There were a number of nasal cowboy standards, including *When My Blue Moon Turns to Gold Again* and *San Antonio Rose*. There were several old Bing Crosby records: *White Christmas* and *Don't Fence Me In*. There were a number of year-old blues sides, featuring honking one-note saxes and leering pseudo-sexual lyrics leading up to inevitable anticlimaxes. There was a haphazard collection of middle-aged hit-parade agonies, notably *Doggie in the Window* and *Till I Waltz Again with You*. And finally, slipped in by mistake, there was an old Benny Goodman Sextet number, *Rose Room*. He played that ten times during the first week, and then gave up.

In a way he could not quite understand, the record had violated an unseen pattern. It was not a simple and obvious case of the record's being out of place in Jefferson Springs; rather, it was the fact that music was being played at all, *any* music. The pattern was a subtle one, but he had been trained to be sensitive to just such cultural harmonies and configurations.

Paul Ellery had often remarked elsewhere that he would just as soon eat his food without the collective sobbings of the music industry in the background, to say nothing of an endless babble of human voices earnestly reciting the current cliches. Now that he found himself faced with total silence, however, he found the experience unexpectedly unpleasant. The silence cut him off, isolated him. It put him in the middle of a bright stage, without a script or an orchestra, alone, with the curtain going up.

He sat for what seemed to him to be a long time, smoking his pipe. Somehow, only fifteen slow minutes crawled by on the greasy electric clock above the doorway. The doorway led to a small alcove, which faced both the kitchen and the dark, deserted beer bar. He listened closely, but could hear nothing. The other door led outside, into the town.

He was afraid to go out.

He shoved back his chair and got to his feet, annoyed with himself. He told himself that there was nothing to fear. He remembered a time many years before, when he was just a kid. He had gone to a midnight show with another boy to see *Son of Frankenstein*. Then he had had to walk home, through the city of Austin. He and the other boy had walked all the way back to back, one walking frontward and the other backward, in order to keep an eye peeled in both directions at once. It wasn't that they *believed* in such things, of course, it wasn't that they were afraid——

You know.

It was that way now. What was he afraid of? No one had tried to harm him in Jefferson Springs. After all, it was just a little Texas town, just like a thousand others drowsing on the highway or tucked away on a back road, wasn't it? *Wasn't it?*

He left a dollar bill and two quarters on the damp table and walked out of the cafe. After the gloomy humidity of the dining room, the dry heat outside was a tonic. It wasn't cool yet by a long shot, and the sidewalk was still warm under his feet, but the burning sun had gone down. There was even the ghost of a breeze rustling in from the desert and trying to work its way down the street.

He stood in front of the whitewashed cafe and considered. He was a big man, standing a shade under six feet and pushing two hundred pounds. His brown eyes were shrewd and steady. He was dressed in the local uniform—khaki shirt and trousers, capped with a warped, wide-brimmed felt hat at one end and cowboy boots at the other. His Ph.D. didn't show, and he didn't look like the kind of a man who had often been frightened.

Jefferson Springs waited for him quietly. The cafe was at the northern end of the town, on Main Street. Main Street was split down the middle by the railroad, with its little station and loading platforms. Orange trees were planted on both sides of the tracks. To his right, two blocks away, he could see the lights of the Rialto, where a Mitzi Gaynor movie was now in progress. There were a few street lights, a few passing cars moving very slowly, but Jefferson Springs was dark and shadow-crossed.

Jefferson Springs. To the casual onlooker, it was nothing. A place to drive through on your way to the city. A place to get gas, if you were lucky enough to find a station open after dark.

Paul Ellery knocked the ashes out of his pipe against the curb. He had read many books written by men in search of the unknown, the mysterious. They had looked in the Arctic. They had looked in the jungles of South America. They had looked in Africa, in Egypt, in Polynesia. They had taken telescopes and spectroscopes and looked out into space, at the moon, at Mars, at Jupiter, at the stars beyond. They had invented the electroencephalograph and had looked in the human brain.

No one had ever looked in Jefferson Springs. Jefferson Springs was no place to look for the unknown. How known could you get?

Paul Ellery had spent the summer in Jefferson Springs. He hadn't merely lived there—he had studied the town. He had made schedules and charts and investigations, because that was his job. He had asked questions and checked up on the answers. He had read the paper, examined the records, interviewed the people. He had looked at Jefferson Springs the way he would at an Eskimo settlement or an African village.

And Jefferson Springs didn't add up. Jefferson Springs wasn't what it seemed to be. Jefferson Springs was—different. Unknown? You could call it that, all right, and more.

He looked up and down the street. There was not a single human in sight. He walked around the corner slowly, and got into his car, a Ford. He stuck the key in the ignition and just sat there, not knowing where to go. He was beaten, and had he been anyone else he would have admitted the fact and gone his way. Paul Ellery, however, was a stubborn man.

"The joint is jumping," he said aloud, staring at the empty town. "I wonder what's doing down at the morgue."

The stars were coming out above him now. He could smell the fragrance of the orange trees along the railroad tracks. It was a lonely smell, and a nostalgic one. It made him think of Anne, less than two hundred miles away in Austin. Two hundred miles—that was four hours' driving time. If he left now, he could be there a little after midnight. And why not? What was he accomplishing here?

But he knew he wouldn't go. He couldn't go, not yet. Not until he knew.

He had read a few lines, years ago, that had intrigued

him enough to start him out on a career. He thought of them now, as he had thought of them many times the past two months in Jefferson Springs

The fact is, like it or not, that we know more about the Crow Indians than we do about the average citizen of the United States. We know more about Samoan villages than we do about American cities. We know a thousand times as much about the Eskimos as we do about the people who live in the small towns of the so-called civilized world. Who lives there, in those unexplored communities we drive through on our way to and from the great cities? What do they do, what do they think, where do they come from, where are they going?

A shocking handful of small American villages have been scientifically studied by cultural anthropologists and rural sociologists. The sample is so small as to be meaningless. The data are hopelessly inadequate. We know as much about the planet Mars as we do about ninety-nine per cent of our own country.

Look at the towns and villages and whistle-stops of America. Go into them with your eyes open, take nothing for granted, and study them as objectively as you would a primitive tribe. There is no man on this planet who can predict what you may find.

Well, he had found plenty, if he could only put it all together and make some kind of sense out of it. He had found more than the author of those lines had ever dreamed of.

He started the motor, cut in the lights, and began to drive aimlessly through the dark streets. He made the long square of Main Street first, not sure what he was looking for, not even sure he wanted to find it.

He drove down past the drugstore, which was open but deserted, past the bank and the dry-goods store and the jewelry shop and the Rialto. The Rialto was bright with lights, and he caught a fragment of tinny music and deep, mechanical voices as he drove by. There was a girl sitting in the glass ticket booth, doing her nails.

He turned left, bouncing across the railroad tracks, and then left again down the other side of Main Street. It was much the same, with minor variations: another drug store, this one closed, a Humble gas station, an "American Club" that was actually a combination pool hall and domino parlor, the Hot Chili Cafe, a grocery store, a few houses, and the Catholic Church. He turned left again at the big, square icehouse, jounced across the tracks, and looked over into the Mexican section of town. There was a little more life there—a few scattered lights, a woman laughing somewhere, the faint strumming of a guitar.

Paul Ellery pulled up along the curb, put the Ford in neutral, and left the motor running. He refilled his pipe and lit it. He didn't want to go back to his hotel room at the Rocking-T. He just couldn't face another long night of sitting alone and wrestling with the senseless data he had got in Jefferson Springs.

He constructed a newspaper headline for his own amusement: YOUNG SCIENTIST BAFFLES LEARNED SOCIETIES; MIXES FACTS IN LABORATORY AND GETS NOTHING.

He noticed that his hands were sweating, and it wasn't that hot now. He tried to analyze his fear. Partly, it was the result of two months of overt and covert hostility from Jefferson Springs. Partly, it was the result of working on a research grant and not coming up with the right dope. Partly, it was the pattern that always just eluded him—the pattern that would make sense of his charts and files and statistics.

Mostly, it was a feeling. He had lived in Texas all his life, except for a stretch in the army and two years at the University of Chicago. He knew his state pretty well. It was a diverse state, despite all the stereotypes. The coastal city of Galveston was utterly unlike the capital city of Austin, just as booming Houston was quite different from Abilene or Amarillo or Fort Worth or Laredo. Nevertheless, happily or otherwise, a man knew when he was in Texas.

Jefferson Springs didn't belong. It wasn't quite Texas. It wasn't even quite America. In fact, it wasn't quite——

What was he thinking of?

"Cut that out, boy," he said to himself. "You're headed for the funny factory."

He made up his mind. He wasn't going back to the hotel, not yet. Somewhere, there had to be the clue he needed. Somewhere, there had to be an answer. Somewhere—but where?

There was one possibility.

He cut the car into gear and drove back along Main Street, and on out of town. He drove south, along the highway that led eventually to Eagle Pass and Mexico, toward the Nueces River. The land was flat but rolling, and his headlights picked out the dark twistings of mesquite trees and brush. The night was almost cool now, and the breeze slanting in from the window vents was fresh and crisp. The Ford hummed along the empty highway. Ahead of him, the lights stabbed a path through the early darkness. Behind him, the night shadows flowed in again and filled up the hole.

Paul Ellery knew, with complete certainty, that there was something terribly wrong with the town of Jefferson Springs. He meant to find out what it was.

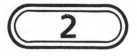

2

FIVE MILES OUTSIDE of town, he turned off the highway to the left. The car purred along, still on a paved road, with plowed fields on either side. The stars were coming out above him.

Trying to calm himself, he switched on the car radio. The faded yellow light on the dial clicked on, together with a vast humming. Ellery hadn't been able to afford the standard radio when he had bought the car, so he had installed a special model he had found on sale. It had its drawbacks, but it worked. It warmed up and the first thing he got, naturally, was one of the huckster stations with mailing addresses in Texas and transmitters in Mexico, where they could pour on the power:

Yes sir, friends, I want to remind you again tonight of our big special offer. My daughter and I are offering you absolutely the biggest hymn book you've ever seen. This beautiful book, which will give you hours and days of pleasure and consolation, is two feet high and one foot wide. Yes sir, that's feet we're talking about—and remember that there are twelve inches in every single foot. And now, before my daughter sings one of these grand old hymns for you, just let me mention the price of this huge hymn book. The price is the best part of all, my friends, and remember that it's your contributions that keep this faith broadcast on the air——

Ellery tried again, and picked up a network show out of a San Antonio station:

(Burst of crashing music.) *Oh ho! And our next contestant, whose name is Ambrose Earnest, is from none other than Sulfur Creek, Colorado!* (Wild applause.) *Well now, Mr. Earnest, you're not nervous are you?* (Laughter) *Oh ho! Now then,¯ Mr. Earnest, for two hundred and sixty-eight dollars in new quarters, can you tell me under what name William Frederick Cody became famous in the West?* (Long pause) *What's that? Speak right up, please. Oh ho, I'm sorry—Billy the Kid is not the correct answer.* (Moan) *But we don't want you to go away yet——*

Ellery turned the radio off. Nevertheless, his mood had brightened considerably. It was all so utterly prosaic—the peaceful country road, the night, the radio. How could there be subtle terror in a world of two-foot-high hymn books? How could there be horror in the land of Ambrose Earnest from Sulfur Creek, Colorado?

He rumbled across the old bridge that spanned the Nueces, and turned sharply to the right along the river. The road was gravel now, and his tires crunched through the ruts, although there was no need to slow down. A screen of trees blocked his view of the Nueces on his right, and a fenced pasture stretched away into the darkness on his left. He was getting close to the ranch road.

What was there, really, that alarmed him in Jefferson Springs? Paul Ellery told himself that he was neither wildly imaginative nor given to flights of occult speculation. He was an anthropologist working on a community study, and he had experience both as a teacher and as a research scientist.

Apart from his profession, he was skeptical by temperament. He liked facts and was apt to ask embarrassing questions to get them. He had a habit of being right, and a rather poor memory for the few times he had been wrong. This led him to a certain cynical bullheadedness, which wasn't as objectionable as it might have been, because he was saved by a lively sense of humor and a pleasant, unpretentious personality.

In any event, he wasn't given to seeing ghosts.

Okay. Rule out the supernatural. Chins up, and all that rot. How could he explain the facts?

ITEM: When he had first chosen Jefferson Springs as the subject for a community study, and had got a grant from the Norse Fund in New York to carry it out, he had met with nothing but hostility from the inhabitants of the town. When that happened, in ordinary circumstances, an anthropologist with only a few months for research usually picked out another town where he could get quicker returns for the time invested. Ellery, however, had been stubborn. He wasn't to be licked by Jefferson Springs.

ITEM: After a few weeks, the people had changed their tactics. Instead of clamming up, they had talked willingly and volubly. They had told him everything. Unfortunately, hardly a word of what they said rang true.

ITEM: There was not one single person in the town of Jefferson Springs who had lived there longer than fifteen years. The town had a population of six thousand. Now, Jefferson Springs, for all its woebegone appearance to a stranger, was no ghost town. It had been continuously occupied for one hundred and thirty-two years. There had been no disasters, no social upheavals, no plagues, no crop failure, no nothing.

ITEM: That meant, in a nutshell, that the entire population—six thousand men, women, and children—had been *replaced*. What other word was there to use? The original citizens, one by one, had moved out. The last had left only a few years ago. At the same time, different people had moved in. None of them had been there longer than fifteen years, and most of them had lived in Jefferson Springs a much shorter time than that. It was a totally new population.

ITEM: In view of the average Texan's devotion to his land and his town; in view of the old families who lived in all such small towns, resolutely facing the past; in view of a million things this unexplained shift in population was impossible.

ITEM: But there it was. What do your learned books have to say on the subject? Nothing? How sad.

ITEM: The culture of Jefferson Springs, as described to him by informants after everyone had decided to talk, was a lovely textbook example of a typical Texas small town. Everything was in precisely the right place and in the right amounts. It was exactly as though you had read that three out of four men wore chlorophyll bags in their ears, and then you went out into a busy street and there they were. One, two, three men with chlorophyll bags; one without, doubtless self-conscious. One, two, three men with chlorophyll bags; one without. As regular as clockwork. And as phony as hell.

ITEM: The people of Jefferson Springs just didn't *feel* right. Paul Ellery was ready to swear that they were not the genuine article. They said the right things at the right times, and more or less did the right things at the right times. But it wasn't spontaneous. They were play-acting. The stage setting was absolutely authentic, and they had all memorized their lines. But the play was a fraud. It was a soap opera with no soap.

ITEM: *Why?*

He came to the Thorne Ranch gate and stopped the car. He left his headlights on, got out, and slid the wooden bar back to release the gate. He pushed it back and drove the car through, then rode the gate back shut and fastened it again. The night was very still. Except for the frogs down along the Nueces, croaking their ancient song, and the gentle breeze sighing across the fields, there wasn't a sound. The stars were bright now, and diamond-hard. There was no moon.

He eased the Ford along the dirt ranch road, taking it slow. When he had gone almost a mile, he topped a small rise and looked down on the buildings of the Thorne Ranch ahead of him. They were completely dark, without a light on anywhere. Either everyone was asleep or away, or else they could see in the dark. It was an indication of Ellery's frame of mind that he rather favored the latter view. As a matter of fact, he had noticed that there were far too few lights burning in Jefferson Springs at night. The town was kept dark, and once you got off the main highway it was exceptional to see a lighted window after eight or nine o'clock. What did that mean, if anything? Was it significant?

He stopped the car, pulling into the rut by the side of the road. Trying to organize his thoughts, he cut the motor and turned off his lights. Whatever was going on at the Thorne Ranch, he had neither excuse nor authority for prowling around the grounds in the dark. His mission was hardly urgent enough to rout Thorne out of bed—or was it? How could he tell? He would have liked to examine the grounds further, just on the off-chance of picking up something useful, but that was a good way to stop a bullet on any ranch, mysterious or not.

He was reluctant to turn back. There was no place to go. He sat and listened to the frogs, welcoming their familiar music. He watched the stars, clean in the smoke-free air.

Melvin Thorne was a big, gruff, soft-spoken Texan. Correction: *appeared* to be. Ellery wasn't taking anything on faith anymore. Nobody, he decided, ever questioned the obvious. Therefore, if you were trying to put a fast one over, the obvious was a good place to start.

Thorne was something of a leader in Jefferson Springs— neither rich nor poor, but a man who commanded respect. He had been cordial enough to Ellery when Ellery had interviewed him, and had urged him to drop in again. He had even made the more or less inevitable suggestion that when Ellery got tired of fooling around with all them books he could always get an honest job on the Thorne Ranch.

The stuff that Thorne had told him about the ranch was average information, and absolutely identical with the information given him by Jim Walls, who had the place out near Comanche Lake. As usual, it was *too* identical. It was a carbon copy.

Ellery had decided to try an experiment. He would fake all the data given him by Walls, making it flatly contradict what Thorne had told him of ranching conditions, and then ask Thorne to explain the discrepancies. It wasn't much, but it might be a lead.

He sat in the darkness, feeling a little foolish. It was all so incongruous, really. That was one thing that made the whole problem so tough: it didn't *look* like a problem. You had to go back constantly to your notes to make certain it was really there, and not just a figment of imagination, or a rationalization for sloppy work. The setting was all wrong for a mystery—no dark castles, no murders, no thunder and lightning, no mad scientist, no beautiful girl.

Just a soft summer night on a country road. Just a sleepy ranch and frogs by the river. Just earth and air and stars.

It was then that he got the feeling.

He couldn't place it at first. He sat up straight, suddenly tense. He held the steering wheel tightly in his hands, ready to move. What was wrong?

He listened. There was only the breeze, and the frogs in the distance.

He looked. There was the ranch, dark and deserted. There was the land around him. There was the night, frosted with stars.

And something else.

He held his breath. His heart thudded in his throat. He looked up, above the outbuildings of the Thorne Ranch, into the night sky.

There was something there—something enormous.

Paul Ellery released his breath in a hissing whisper. He felt the cold sweat pop out on his forehead and his hands felt sticky on the plastic of the steering wheel. Very quietly, he opened the door of his Ford and stepped out on the dirt road. Free from the distortion effect of the windshield, he looked up again.

The thing was still there.

Actually, it wasn't what he *saw* that frightened him. It was what he *didn't* see. He couldn't really see the thing at all, but he could feel its presence in the skies.

His neck ached but he kept his head back, staring. It was a perfectly clear night—he must remember that. There wasn't a cloud in the sky. The moon was just rising, but it was still swelling on the horizon and did not interfere with his line of sight. There were millions of stars burning in the darkness.

Except, of course, where they were blotted out.

That was what he saw. There was a dark mass in the sky over his head that covered up the stars. He could trace its outlines without difficulty, but he could not actually *see* it, apart from an occasional dull glint of reflected light. Its outlines were long and slender, rather pointed at one end, rounded off at the other. It was difficult to judge, because he could not tell for certain what its altitude was, but he roughly estimated its length as at least five hundred yards. It hung in the sky, completely motionless. It neither threatened nor promised. It was just there.

Paul Ellery did not know how long he stood in the dirt road, but it was a long time. Finally, he was rewarded by a flash of muted flame under the cylindrical shadow. A small shadow detached itself from the larger one, and started to float down. Unmistakably, it was headed for the Thorne Ranch.

Ellery's first impulse was to run. He felt utterly helpless, utterly alone. Worst of all, he felt insignificant. But he stood his ground. This was his chance. It he let it go by, he would never sleep soundly again. If he took advantage of it——

He stood very still, watching.

He could see the descending shape fairly clearly now. It was spherical, featureless, about ten feet in diameter. It looked like nothing so much as a huge metal beach ball.

It landed without a sound in the yard of the ranch house, not a quarter of a mile from Ellery's Ford. Five figures got out of it. They didn't speak. In the light of the rising moon, he saw that one of them, unmistakably, was the rancher, Melvin

Thorne. The other four, at least at that distance, were strangers to Ellery—a man and a woman and two children. They went into the ranch house and closed the door behind them. Surprisingly, they turned a light on.

The metal globe hummed very slightly and floated back into the air, where it rejoined the massive shadow above. There was a flicker of light, so brief that Ellery could hardly be sure that he had seen it, and that was all.

The shadow in the sky was gone. The stars looked down on him, twinkling.

Paul Ellery got back into his car and carefully closed the door. He was completely stunned, and it took a real effort to keep his hands from trembling. He looked at his watch. It was half-past ten.

He couldn't think. Nothing made sense to him, not now. The most important thing in the world to him at that moment was to get his mind back on the tracks. He had to make some sanity out of the world in which he found himself—a different world, surely, than the one he had thought he knew. Otherwise, he was just an animal—a rat in a maze.

It might be that he was not entirely rational that night. He had been through a lot, and subtle pressures can sometimes build up and explode with frightening violence. He had always thought of himself as an essentially practical man. Certainly he was not the hero type. And yet——

He had been treated like a fool. He didn't like it.

He clamped an iron grip on his mind, refusing to panic. He started the engine. He turned his headlights on bright. Making plenty of noise, he drove straight down the dirt road toward the ranch house. He would have to do it some time, or go crazy.

He had driven out here tonight to ask Melvin Thorne some questions, and that was what he was going to do.

3

ELLERY KNOCKED ON the door. There was a long heart-beat while the world held its breath. Then heavy footsteps thudded along from inside the house, coming toward the door.

The door opened.

Melvin Thorne stood there in the yellow frame of light. He could not have looked less mysterious. He was a big man, bigger than Ellery. He stood a good six-feet-three, and he was solid. He might have weighed two hundred and twenty pounds, and it was all rock-hard. His hair was brown and thinned down against his skull as a result of years of wearing a hat to shade his pale eyes from the sun. He was dressed in style—khaki trousers, light shirt with the throat open, boots. He needed a shave.

A *perfect imitation*, thought Ellery.

"Howdy, Paul," said Melvin Thorne. His voice was slow and friendly, and the drawl was unmistakable. "What can I do for you this time of night?"

Easy now. Take it slow.

19

"I'd like to ask you a few more questions, Mr. Thorne, if
you could spare me a few minutes."

"My name is Mel," said Melvin Thorne. He paused.
"Kinda late," he suggested.

"I know this is a poor time to come calling, Mel, but I
surely would appreciate your help. I'm running into some
things that are like to tying me in knots."

"Well, now, Paul, that would be a shame."

Ellery said nothing. His hands were wet with sweat.

"Well, come along in, son," Thorne said, smiling.
"Reckon a few minutes won't hurt none."

Ellery followed Thorne inside the house, and Thorne
locked the door behind him. Ellery pretended not to notice—
why shouldn't a man lock the door in his own home? Why
shouldn't a *man*—

The house seemed deserted; Ellery couldn't see a sign of
the four people who had come in with Thorne from the
sphere. He listened, but all he heard was the sound of his
own footsteps and a big, noisy clock ticking in the living
room. The house was typical of small Texas ranch houses,
which meant that it resembled a standard frame farm house.
There were no wagon wheels, buffalo rugs, or brands on the
furniture. The rooms were comfortable, but hardly flamboy-
ant. It was a clean, middle-class, town-on-Saturday, church-
on-Sunday house. It had a no-nonsense air about it.

Thorne led him into the kitchen, of course. There was
the big farm icebox in the corner, the big iron stove against
the wall, the shelves of mugs and plain dishes, the battered
wood table with a fresh red-and-white checked table cloth.
They sat down at the table. There were salt and pepper
shakers on the table, each of which was inscribed with a
deathless bit of verse. The salt shaker said: "I'm full of SALT,

all nice and white; some use me heavy, some use me light."
The pepper shaker said: "I'm full of PEPPER, don't shake me
a lot; use me sparingly, I'm pretty hot."

Mystery?

"Coffee?" asked Melvin Thorne.

Ellery nodded. "Please," he said.

Thorne poured from the big black pot on the stove.
Where did the coffee come from? Paul Ellery wondered. *There
hadn't been time to make any fresh.*

Ellery drank it black. It was warm, but not really hot. He
decided that Thorne must have just turned the fire on under
the old coffee when he had heard the knock on the door.

Thorne made a face. "Coffee's right poor," he said. "The
missus hasn't been feeling none too well lately. Anyhow, you
know how women are—they all like weak coffee. Now *I*
always say the more coffee the better. You're not drinkin' the
stuff to taste the *water.*"

"That's sure right," Ellery agreed, searching for an opening. What could he say to this man? *By the way, Mel, I've
just been wondering—are you a Martian?*

That would hardly do.

"Well, son," Thorne said, "start firin' in those questions
of yours. I can't read your mind, you know."

Paul Ellery looked at him sharply, but the other's face was
smiling and unsuggestive.

It was very quiet in the house. The big clock ticked in the
living room, and that was all. Four people had come inside
with Thorne, had come down out of the sky. Where were
they? Hiding behind the door? Under the bed? In a secret
passage?

Absurd. It was all absurd. And the ship——

Ellery licked his lips slowly. He was good and tired of

beating around the bush. He was afraid and uncertain and confused, for the first time in his life, but he knew he had two choices in Jefferson Springs: he could go on with the farce, write up the data he knew to be false, and go on his way; or, if he dared, he could go after the truth, no matter where it led him.

He smiled. He knew that he had no choice at all. "Mel," he said, "I need your help."

Thorne poured more coffee for himself and refilled Ellery's cup. This time, it was steaming hot, and a big improvement over the first batch.

"Happy to help out, son," Thorne said. "'Course, I don't claim to know nothing about all this stuff of yours, but I know Jefferson Springs as well as the next man and better than some."

Ellery nodded, feeling his way. "Look here, Mel, did you ever notice anything—well, strange—peculiar, about Jefferson Springs?"

"I'm not real sure I follow you there."

"Don't you?"

"Well now, you take that Pebbles woman, lives over there by the high school. I'd be the last man in the world to say that woman was *crazy*, but it's a fact that she's plumb peculiar. Now, I recollect one time, I was driving along in my pick-up, and I looked over thataway, and there she is, in broad daylight, pushing that old lawn-mower of hers, and she was plain naked, naked as the day she was born——"

"I don't mean that kind of peculiar, Mel."

"Well, you're dealing this hand. What kind of peculiar *do* you mean?"

Ellery retreated to his favorite defense mechanism—his pipe. He was smoking too much these days, but it gave him a chance to collect his thoughts and look occupied when he wasn't really doing anything. Anyhow, the most mundane statement took on a certain profundity when it was pushed around the stem of a briar. He lit it, broke the match, and dropped it into his wet saucer.

"Here's the kind of peculiar I mean, Mel," he said slowly.

"You ever been anywhere where things just didn't feel right, even when you couldn't quite put your finger on what was wrong? I remember one time—wasn't far from here, either, up around Sabinal—I was riding a one-eyed white mare down the road one afternoon, just as calm and peaceful as you please. Well, all of a sudden that mare shied away from her blind side so quick she almost jerked me out of the saddle, and the next thing I knew she took off like a bat out of hell. Took me a good ten minutes to stop that mare."

Thorne laughed "Nothin' to it," he said. "She seen a snake or something on her blind side and it scared her. Happens all the time."

"Suppose," suggested Paul Ellery, "that there was no snake there? Suppose there was nothing there?"

Thorne shrugged. "So she was jumpy, son. What's peculiar about that? Don't *you* never get jumpy?"

"Sometimes," Ellery admitted. He looked evenly at the man who sat across the table from him. "I've had a funny feeling about Jefferson Springs almost ever since I got here," he said. "In fact, it's more than a feeling. I'm absolutely positive there's something wrong with this town."

"Wrong?" There was a long silence. "With Jefferson Springs?"

"You've never noticed it, I suppose."

"Can't say as I have. Course, there's Mayor Cartwright. I've heard tell the man's a little slippery, but he's a politician, after all. You take that mess in Washington now—I'm not too surprised at anything I might see here at home."

Ellery blew an uncertain smoke ring at the salt shaker. Clearly, he wasn't going to trick Thorne into saying anything revealing. The man was refusing to talk about anything important. And he was a good actor, no doubt about that. Already, despite what he had seen, Ellery began to feel unsure of himself.

Well, he'd just have to get blunter—hit him over the head with it and see what happened. No one had tried to harm him yet in Jefferson Springs, and until they did he meant to keep digging.

He leaned forward. "Cards on the table now, Mel," he said evenly. "I was parked down the road in my Ford when you came home tonight."

The silence deepened. Outside, the summer wind whispered across the land.

Melvin Thorne didn't bat an eye. "What's that got to do with it?"

Ellery took a deep breath. "You came down out of the sky," he said. The words bounced around the prosaic ranch kitchen, trying to find a place to fit.

"I don't follow you, son, not at all. What might you be trying to say?"

"Four other people were with you," Ellery went on doggedly, "a man, a woman, and two children. They came into this house."

Melvin Thorne grinned, big and confident and completely at his ease. "Is this a game, Paul, or have you been hitting the old bottle? Come down out of the *sky!*"

Ellery kept talking. He felt as though he were on a treadmill and couldn't get off. "You came down in a metal sphere. I saw you. What's it all about?"

Ellery felt like a fool, like a complete sap. *Yes, that's the way you're supposed to feel. That's the best defense in the world—the fear of ridicule.*

"You can't be serious. More coffee?"

"Thanks. I'm serious. Damn it, you *know* I'm serious!"

Thorne laughed. "Sphere? Ain't no sphere in *my* yard. Got a old oil drum out in the shed yonder, if that'll help any."

Laugh it up, buddy, Ellery thought, getting mad. *Make with the truisms and the phony accent.* "Stuff a cold and starve a fever," he said. "Still water runs deep. All that glitters is not gold."

Thorne looked at him with concern in his pale eyes. "You're not making very good sense, Paul."

"Neither are you."

"No call to get riled up. I tell you what—if you think there's one of these spheres in my yard, why don't we just go outside and have a look? If you find one, you can keep it and take it home with you."

"I didn't *say* it was in your yard now. I said you came down here in it. I said you came down with four other people out of the sky. Don't humor me, Mel. I know what I saw."

Thorne shrugged. "Anything you say, son. I might as well tell you the truth, since you already know part of it." He smiled. "Fact is, I been herdin' my cattle from a flying saucer. Traded in my jeep and my ridin' stock and bought one out of a mail-order catalogue. They're right nice, too, exceptin' that I always fall off when I try to do any ropin'."

"Cut it out, Mel," Ellery said.

"It was your idea, son. I was just trying to give you some more good ideas."

"I'm mighty grateful." Paul Ellery got to his feet, his fists clenched. He looked the big man in the eye. "I want you to know something, though."

Melvin Thorne got to his feet also. "Yes?"

"I want you to know that I don't believe one damned thing I've heard since I walked into this house. I don't believe one damned thing I've heard since I got to Jefferson Springs. I don't *believe* in Jefferson Springs. I saw you get out of some kind of metal sphere tonight, right out there in your yard, and I saw the ship up above it too. I don't know what the hell is going on around here, but I mean to find out. I don't take kindly to being treated like a two-year-old. I want you to know I'm not leaving this town until I know the score, if it takes me the rest of my life. And spare me the Texas drawl, what say? It stinks."

The big man looked at him. "I'd say you got powerful bad manners, son. I don't know what they're teachin' in the schools these days, but it sure ain't neighborliness."

"Can it," Ellery said. "You're not fooling anybody."

The two men stared at each other across the kitchen table.

Somewhere, far out on the range, a coyote cried.

Melvin Thorne laughed, abruptly. It was a big laugh, a loud laugh. It rebounded around the room, sure and confident and unconcerned.

"I like you, Paul," Mel Thorne said. "You oughta give up them books before you go completely loco, and come and work for me."

Paul Ellery felt tears of helpless rage well up in his eyes. How could you fight an enemy who refused to act like an enemy? How could you deal with a man who refused to meet you on any terms except his own? He measured the man before him carefully.

"Steady," said Melvin Thorne calmly. "You better run along home before you do something foolish. You'll feel better in the morning."

Paul Ellery was not inexperienced, and had been a competent-enough athlete in his time. He wasn't in really poor condition, but Mel Thorne could probably tear him apart if he felt so inclined. He knew the type. Socking him on the jaw would be like kicking a tank in a moment of irritation.

"Okay, Mel," he said. "Thanks for the coffee."

"You're surely welcome," said Melvin Thorne. "Come back any old time."

He led him back through the living room to the front door, unlocked it, and saw him out. The door closed behind him and the lock clicked.

Paul Ellery looked at his watch. A quarter to twelve. Less than four hours ago, he had been finishing up his meal in the Jefferson Springs Cafe.

He walked over to his Ford and got in. He started up the motor and turned around in the dirt drive. His brain spinning, he started back toward town.

It was still a beautiful night, soft and clear and sprinkled with stars. The moon had climbed high above him now, like a great pale eye in the darkness. Everything was so normal it hurt. The frogs were still croaking down along the Nueces, in splendid unconcern. Maybe that was the answer: be a frog.

It was, Paul Ellery thought, like a movie in a nightmare. The people didn't go with the scenery, and the dialogue didn't go with the plot.

What *was* the plot?

He drove fast, and he did not look back.

4

THE NEXT DAY was exactly like the previous sixty-two: hot.

The blazing white sun hung in the sky, almost motionless, as though it too were too hot to move. No cloud braved that furnace, and the heat beat down like boiled, invisible rain. Heat waves shimmered like glass in the still air and the parched earth took on the consistency of forgotten pottery.

Jefferson Springs, from the coolest corner in the thick, square icehouse to the baked metal of the top of the water tower, held its breath and waited for evening.

In his room at the Rocking-T, Paul Ellery sweated. His room was an uninspired boxlike affair, and the resemblance to an oven was more than fleeting. He sat on the thin, plain bed and nursed a pitcher of ice water from the drug store three doors down. His notebooks were scattered over the floor in unscholarly confusion, liberally sprinkled with spilled tobacco. The morning paper, from San Antonio, was stuffed in the wastebasket, and the symbolism was intentional.

He was trying to think. The heat didn't help, and neither

did the events of the preceding night. But he knew the trouble now, knew it clearly: the whole situation was completely outside human experience. The human mind is so constructed that it works on past experiences; these are the data which it tries to utilize. Human beings store up past experiences, both those of the individual and those of the group, and carry them as integral parts of cultures. When a man runs up against a situation, even a novel one for him, he doesn't really have to deal with it alone. He has at least *heard* of such situations, he at least has *some* facts he can bring to bear, he at least has *some* notion of how to proceed.

Most situations, that is.

Not this one.

This one was unique. In a nutshell, that meant he had to figure it out for himself. That sounds easy enough, being one of the familiar figures of speech of the English language, but Paul Ellery knew that it was not so simple. Most people live and die without ever having to solve a totally new problem. Do you wonder how to make the bicycle stay up? Daddy will show you. Do you wonder how to put the plumbing in your new house? The plumber will show you. Would it be all right to pay a call on Mrs. Layne, after all that scandal about the visiting football player? Well, call up the girls and talk it over. Should you serve grasshoppers at your next barbecue? Why, nobody does that. Shall you come home from the office, change to a light toga, and make a small sacrifice in the back yard? What would the neighbors think!

But—how do you deal with a Whumpf in the butter?

What do you do about Grlzeads on the stairs?

How much should you pay for a new Lttangnuffel?

Is it okay to abnakave with a prwaatz?

Why, how silly! I never heard of such things. I have enough problems of my own without bothering my head about such goings on. A Whumpf in the butter! I declare.

A *situation completely outside human experience.*

Paul Ellery could see just how lovely the situation would appear from the other side of the fence. If you wish to devise a problem that cannot be solved, the simplest way is to make it appear that there *is* no problem. So long as everyone is convinced that all the answers are on file, nobody bothers to devise new answers. And if the problem is so constructed that you cannot even accept it as real without doubting your own sanity——?

How *could* the Earth go around the Sun? Any fool could see that it was the other way around, just by watching. How *could* there be anything alien and inexplicable in a little Texas town right on the San Antonio highway? Any fool could drive through it and see that it was just like any other town.

But when you introduced astronomy and mathematics——

Or anthropology and community-study techniques——

Paul Ellery frowned at his scattered notebooks. It was all there, the whole pat, unbelievable story.

There was the expected class structure, ranging from "that no-good trash" through the various ethnic groups to "those big shots who think they're better than anyone else." The pattern was closer to what West reported from Plainville than to Warner's elaborate class divisions from Yankee City, but that was in line with the size of the communities involved.

There was the expected emphasis on the high school as an upward-mobility mechanism. Clyde Kluckhohn and others had long ago pointed out that education had tended to supplant the frontier as a pet way to get along in the world, and this seemed to be as true in Jefferson Springs as else-where. Americans expected their children to get a better deal than they had, and the high school was usually the ladder that led upstairs.

There were the expected racial stereotypes about Negroes and Mexicans, and it was depressing to see that so little had changed since Powdermaker had written her *After Freedom* in 1939. There was the expected rural-urban ecology, the expected small-town kin ties, the expected suspicion of "those crooks in Washington."

But, somehow, it didn't fit together into a coherent whole—or more precisely, it fitted together *too* well. The neighborhood maps, the statistics, the symbol systems, the values—they added up to a perfect, ideal "type" that simply could not exist in reality. Social science was one devil of a long way from being that precise in its predictions. No one had ever found an ideal "folk" society as conceptualized by Redfield, and no one could expect to find a community as typical in every way as Jefferson Springs.

Still, he had found one. There were no ragged edges, no individual peculiarities, no human unpredictability.

It was, in a word, faked data.

It was a false face.

The entire population of Jefferson Springs had been replaced within the last fifteen years. Even a superficial look at courthouse records, supplemented with names and dates from Austin, had told him that much. The town had been taken over. The old residents had moved out—under what kind of pressure?

Okay.

Say it. Are you afraid of the words? This little town is in contact with—something—out in space. Thorne knows. They all know.

The cowboy hats and the boots and the Texas drawls and the inane weekly paper meant nothing. They were clothes worn to a costume party. Whose party?

Toward evening, when the intolerable heat eased off to become merely acutely uncomfortable, he left the hotel and endured another meal at the Jefferson Springs Cafe. Whatever the things were he was up against, he reflected, they had certainly learned the secret of Texas cooking: fry it in too much grease, add day-old French-fries, allow to cool, serve on soiled plate. When he had finished, he went back to his hotel.

There were two men in his room.

They were pleasant enough in appearance, quite unsinister, young, and casually dressed in sport clothes. They might have wandered in from a yacht club. One of them smoked a pipe. Ellery had never seen either one of them before.

"Hello, Ellery," said the man with the pipe, as though Ellery had just dropped in for a visit. "I hope we haven't alarmed you by waiting for you here."

"You've scared me to death. So what?"

"The fact is, Ellery, that we'd like to talk to you, if you're not too busy investigating us." He gestured at the notebooks with his pipe. "Interesting reading."

"Thanks," said Ellery. He stuck his hands in his pockets. "Make yourselves at home, gentlemen. My time is your time."

The men hesitated. "We'd rather hoped you'd come with us," offered the one without the pipe finally. "We think we can save you some time, if you're interested."

"I'm interested," Ellery looked them over carefully. "Where are we going?"

The pipe-smoker smiled. "To the ship," he said. "I believe you caught a glimpse of it last night, isn't that correct? I'm sure you'll find it interesting."

Paul Ellery lit a cigarette; he smoked them whenever his pipe got too foul even for him. He felt as though he were caught up on a treadmill, pushed and pulled by forces over which he had no control. And yet, the choice was his. The two men had asked him if he wanted to come along, and seemingly that was what they meant. They had not told him that he *must* go with them.

Strangely, much of his fear had left him. He didn't know whether it was because he was getting used to the situation or because the situation was too implausible to be feared. You can't fear the totally unknown—what you fear is something within your experience that you cannot fully understand but have reason to believe is dangerous.

These people were X factors—unknowns.

Obviously, they were not melodrama villains, twisting their black mustaches while they fed the babies to the meat grinders. They seemed reasonable enough. If Jefferson Springs had wished to harm him, there had been many chances. And if these people had really come from a ship in space, they were probably more intelligent than he was, or at least had far superior knowledge. If they were out to get him, they could deliver the goods at their own convenience. If not——

The ship, up there under the stars.

"Would you object if I carried a gun?" asked Ellery . "You gentlemen are strangers to me, you know."

The man with the pipe shrugged cheerfully. "You'll be perfectly safe with us," he assured him, "but by all means take a gun along if it makes you feel better."

Humor the native, Paul Ellery thought wryly. *If he wants to take his spear, let him take it.*

Well, it would make him feel better. He walked over to the dresser and took his .38 from the middle drawer, where he kept it hidden under his shirts. As a man who had to do a lot of moving around, Ellery kept the revolver with him as a precaution. He checked the cartridges, smiled at the two men who were watching him, and dropped a spare box of ammunition in his pocket. Then he stuck the gun in his belt and changed his shirt to a short-sleeved seersucker, replete with designs of palm trees and improbable dancing girls. He left the shirttail out, which at least served to make the .38 a little less conspicuous.

"Lead on, MacDuff," said Paul Ellery.

The man with the pipe nudged his companion. "That's him," he said, in perfect seriousness. "That's Shakespeare, remember? Misquoted, I believe, from *Macbeth*."

Ellery stared at the man, but said nothing. He switched out the light and followed the two men out of the hotel. The air was pleasant now, dry and warm but invigorating after the blistering sunlight.

They got into a perfectly ordinary black Buick and drove out of town. The two strangers sat in the front seat, leaving Ellery alone in the back. He could have shot them both without any difficulty, but of course he had no reason to— yet. The Buick went the other way from Thorne Ranch, out the San Antonio highway for seven or eight miles, and then veered off to the right along a dirt road. They went two miles on that—Ellery checked the speedometer over the driver's shoulder—and then purred to a stop.

Ellery spotted it instantly.

The big ten-foot globe, looking like a giant metal beach ball, swayed lightly in the middle of a plowed field.

They left the Buick by the side of the road, wriggled under a barbed-wire fence, and walked across the field to the gray sphere. A sliding panel lifted at their approach, and white light spilled out. They stepped inside and the panel closed. There was a sensation of lifting, very much the same as riding in a smooth elevator.

The interior of the globe was unremarkable. It was simply a hollow sphere, with a flat floor section built in, furnished with a soft gray wall-to-wall carpet, and two comfortable green couches. There was a very faint smell of electricity—or something like electricity—in the air. The globe hummed slightly, and there was a barely discernible vibration.

The two men sat on one couch, clearly not thinking about the ride at all. Paul Ellery sat on the other one and tried not to look like a country boy on his first trip to the big city.

His heart was thumping much too fast for his peace of mind, and his blood sang in his ears. What he felt was not fear, nor even wonder. He accepted it, all of it, because there was nothing else he could do. Here he was, and that was that. It was quite beyond his comprehension, and he knew it.

There was no name for what he felt, floating through the night sky with two men who were not of Earth.

The sphere stopped, very gently. There was a muffled thump as something locked into place. The two men stood up, and Ellery followed their example. The sliding panel opened. Outside, there was a glow of subdued yellowish light.

"After you," said the man with the pipe, smiling.

Somehow, Paul Ellery walked through the door. He passed through a short corridor—out of the garage, he thought rather wildly—and then he was inside of it. Inside the great shadow that had blotted out the stars.

Say it. A spaceship.

A long hallway stretched before him, with soothing indirect lighting in the walls. The floor was spotlessly clean and polished. There were panels along the sides, evidently leading to rooms of some sort. What could be in those rooms? How many secrets did this ship hold, secrets as yet unguessed by the men of Earth? Where had this ship been built, and when, and what ports had it seen as it cruised the greatest sea of all?

The hallway ahead was deserted and silent.

They don't want to scare me, he thought. *Caution! Do not frighten the aborigine!*

"Just walk straight ahead," said one of the men behind him. "You have nothing to fear, I assure you."

Paul Ellery walked straight ahead. Superficially, it was not unlike walking along an air-conditioned corridor in some modern skyscraper. Almost, you could imagine that you could stroll over to a window and look out, and there would be the familiar towers and gray, honking streets of a large city.

Except that there weren't any windows.

Except that you were hanging in the air, far above the cities of Earth.

Except that the .38 in your belt suddenly seemed an amusing toy, nothing more.

He walked for what seemed to be a long time, with the

footsteps of the two men clicking behind him in the hallway. Actually, by his watch, it took him a little over one minute.

But it was a long minute.

At the end of the corridor, there was a heavy door, set flush with the wall. There was no knob on it.

"Just go right on in," said the man with the pipe. "The door will open and let you through. We'll be back for you a little later."

The two men turned and walked down the corridor, and disappeared into a branching passage. Paul Ellery was alone.

"Here goes nothing," he said, not giving himself time to hesitate.

He stepped forward and the big door swung open without a sound.

He walked inside.

$$\boxed{5}$$

A LITTLE RED-FACED fat man was waiting for him.
"Ellery!" he exclaimed, extending a stubby hand and getting up from behind a large and untidy desk. "Damn glad to see you—been really looking forward to making your acquaintance. Say, haven't you been the stubborn devil though! I like that, I admire that. Have a drink?"

Paul Ellery got his own hand out in time to have it pumped up and down with enough enthusiasm to make him worry about his shoulder socket. He could not have been more surprised if he had encountered an alligator in a spacesuit. This jovial little fat man simply didn't fit the bill as a mysterious alien. He was about as mysterious as Lassie.

"What the hell," said the fat man, hands on his hips. "Don't stare at me like that, Ellery. This isn't a zoo, old man, and I have always flattered myself on a roughly humanoid appearance."

"Sorry," Paul Ellery managed to say. "I didn't mean to stare. It's just—well, you sort of caught me off base, that's all."

The fat man frowned with what seemed to be genuine

petulance. "What do you want me to do, confound it—act inscrutable or something?"

"Or something," Ellery admitted.

The fat man laughed. "Well, anyhow," he said, "my name here is John. Frightfully original, hey? And now that we've been formally introduced, how about that drink? Permit me to assure you that it is not mere hospitality that speaks—I, the amazing monster from beyond the stars, am thirsty."

Paul Ellery hesitated. This was all coming at him so fast that he hardly knew how to react to it. The behavior pattern just didn't exist. It was just last night that he had stood on the dirt road on the Thorne Ranch, looking up—

But he felt himself relaxing. John seemed an amiable enough old buzzard. At least he wasn't a second-hand Texan, and that was a relief.

Careful. He may be a trick.

"What kind of a drink?" he asked cautiously.

The man called John laughed again. "What kind of a drink? Why, there's only one possibility, of course! I'll let you in on it, because I'm really not John at all—my name is Buster, and I'm an undercover man from the F.B.I.!"

Incredibly, the little fat man began to pace the floor, making wild theatrical passes at the air and frowning hideously. "The drink—ah, yes, the drink. You want to know about the drink?"

Ellery caught himself gaping again. Was the man a lunatic? A—what was the phrase—a mad scientist? Oh no, that would be the last straw! *Call the attendant, Doctor. I'm ready.*

"The drink," announced John, rubbing his small hands

together with great relish, "is none other than a magic potion which will make you our willing slave in our diabolical scheme to turn the Earth into roast beef!"

Ellery laughed out loud, unable to control himself. It sounded a little hysterical.

John abandoned his pose and pretended disgust, but it was evident that he had enjoyed playing his brief role. "Damn it all, Paul," he said, "you're a rational man. You've got to get hold of yourself and calm down. We're banking on your intelligence, old man. Pray don't disappoint us. There's nothing up my sleeve, and I'm not going to turn into a spider and feed you to my young. You chaps, if you don't mind my saying so, have the most monstrous stories about us. There's a whole literature down here that's positively stuffed with invading monsters, ghouls, and a frightfully dull army of dim-witted supermen who dash about through the air thinking at each other and throwing things about with mental force, whatever that is—you read science fiction, of course?"

"Well, no," Ellery admitted. "I haven't had much time for that sort of thing."

John clucked sadly. "Deplorable. The worser sort, that is. Well, no matter. When I say a drink, I mean a *drink*—in your terms, of course. I rather like your Scotch—do you?"

"Yes," said Ellery. "Yes I do, and I could use some." He sat down in a chair in front of the large messy desk. He couldn't pretend to himself that he knew what the score was, but at least he could try not to make a fool of himself.

The little fat man sat down in a plush, padded chair on the other side of the desk and produced a bottle and two glasses from a drawer. The bottle was a familiar one—White Horse. John filled two glasses and handed one to Ellery.

"To sin," he said, and swallowed a good two jiggers in one gulp.

Ellery matched John's drink with one of his own, and the Scotch felt good. He needed it. He looked around the room, trying to get a line on the man who occupied it. The place was jammed with books—all kinds of books. Many of them were totally unfamiliar to him, alien in language and design, but there were others that he had seen before: Thomas Wolfe's *Of Time and the River*, Mark Twain's *Huckleberry Finn*, Ernest Hemingway's *The Sun Also Rises*, A. E. Housman's *A Shropshire Lad*, Thomas Mann's *The Magic Mountain*. Books by Chekhov and Dostoevski, de Maupassant and Sartre, Eliot and Shakespeare. Detective stories by Conan Doyle, Chesterton, Cornell Woolrich. Science fiction by Arthur Clarke, Ray Bradbury, Edgar Pangborn, Clifford Simak. And magazines and newspapers and tapes and cans of film. Ellery even spotted Kroeber's *Anthropology* and Howell's *Mankind So Far*—two books by anthropologists who knew how to write.

"You read a lot," he commented without brilliance.

John grinned and refilled both glasses. "I know you're wondering about many things, Paul."

"Wouldn't you be?"

"Of course." The little man produced a cigarette which glowed into a light when he puffed on it. He frowned. "I'm not playing with you, Paul. I hope you'll excuse my ham acting when you came in—you have no idea how it feels to shake hands with someone and all the time have him look at you as if you were about to sprout wings and squirt fire in his eyes." He drummed his fingers on the untidy desk. Almost, he looked nervous and ill at ease. "You see, Paul, this is rather a ticklish situation. Hard to explain, hard to get across. This isn't easy for me, either. Doing the best I can, do you see?"

Paul Ellery thought he saw. *No use kidding myself. He's the anthropologist and I'm the aborigine.*

"Maybe I can help," he said.

"Maybe you can," John agreed. "I hope you'll try."

"Question one," Ellery said, "what am I doing here?"

John frowned again and puffed on his cigarette. "Look at it this way—and please understand that there is nothing personal in what I say. The fact is that we regard you as an intelligent man. Further, you are a patient man, a persistent man. You even have a basic grounding in the scientific approach to phenomena. All right. You have blundered into a situation, quite by accident, and you've been smart enough to see through the window dressing and formulate a problem. That in itself is remarkable, and we are properly impressed. You are not, frankly, dangerous to us. You *are* a nuisance, if you will excuse my bluntness. Therefore, we have decided to do the only logical thing from our point of view."

"Which is?"

"Remove the nuisance, of course."

Paul Ellery raised his eyebrows. "What do I do—walk the plank?"

John frowned, changed his mind, and laughed. He laughed rather too much for comfort, Ellery thought. But then, he seemed concerned about Ellery's feelngs, not his own. Sincerity, or part of the job? Or both?

"Nonsense," the little fat man said. He tossed his cigarette into a small depression in his desk and the cigarette disappeared. "Utter rot. Our methods are hardly so crude as all that. As a matter of fact, Paul, I can set your mind at ease a bit by telling you one simple fact. It is this: we are forbidden by the laws under which we live to harm physically any native of your planet. Ah, I see this surprises you! You find it hard to imagine that the monsters from space live under laws of their own?"

"To tell you the truth," said Ellery, "I never thought about it."

"Ummm. Well, be that as it may, the fact is that you probably have less to fear from us than from your own people. So do try to relax. You're making *me* nervous."

Paul Ellery savored the Scotch in his mouth. He tried to picture the scene he was enacting: a young man sitting across the table from some sort of an alien, an alien with what almost amounted to an inferiority complex about being an alien, in a spaceship hanging over the Earth, discussing the nuisance value of the aborigines. It wasn't easy to visualize. It was still less easy to accept as reality—it had all happened too fast. But only an idiot could bury his head in the sand and convince himself that what was happening *couldn't* happen.

"Question two," said Paul Ellery. "Are the people in Jefferson Springs—well, human?

John poured more Scotch. He must, Ellery thought, have a capacity like a storage tank. What did they drink where *he* came from?"

"You'll have to define 'human,' I'm afraid, before your question will make much sense," John said, inserting another cigarette in his mouth. "Do you mean, to employ your own terminology, a creature that may be classified as kingdom Animal, phylum Chordata, class Mammal, subclass Eutheria, order Primate, sub-order Anthropoidea, family Hominidae, genus Homo, species sapiens? Do you mean a divine creature with a soul, and do you care to specify any particular religious faith? Do you mean the highest product of evolution? Do you mean people born on Earth, or in America, or perchance in Texas? Do you mean a highly complex animal which, by means of glandular interaction, possesses rare spiritual qualities? Do you mean an essence, a vapor, an ultimate this-or-that? Do you mean something, say, with a cranial capacity of over a thousand cubic centimeters? Do you mean someone with whom you are not at war at the present time?"

Paul Ellery digested that slowly. To cover his own confusion, he resorted again to his pipe, filling it and lighting it with slow deliberation. Whatever else he might be, the little fat man was no fool. All right, then—what did *he* mean by "human?"

"Suppose we rephrase my somewhat childish question," he said. "First of all, as to your physical type, if I can use the term, I should judge that these people are indeed Homo sapiens, at least externally. Right?"

"You have answered your own question," John said. "Isn't it surprising how much you know if you will just stop half a second and think?"

"Okay," Ellery went on. "Next, were you born on Earth? I presume not. Next, if you weren't born on Earth, where *were* you born? More important, are you the product of a completely different evolutionary chain, unconnected in any way with Earth? As an anthropologist, I find it hard to understand how man could be repeated so precisely somewhere else in the universe. The line of development that produced man is so improbable and twisted——"

"If I may say so," John interrupted him, "there are a good many things anthropologists do not understand."

"I would be the last to deny that," Ellery admitted. He felt relaxed now, almost at his ease. It was like a bull session in college—except that college was a spaceship, high above the sleeping Earth.

"No offense, Paul," the fat man assured him. "Anthropologists are no worse than other natives of your planet. In fact, they are less certain than others, which means they are almost on the road to average intelligence. But we digress, my friend. The Scotch has loosened your tongue, and it has made me arrogant."

"It hasn't made you answer my question, however."

"Ummm. Well, it's no secret. The galaxy has spawned man many times, although its motive for doing so, if I may anthropomorphize a bit, seems obscure. In fact, man is a rather common animal. All it seems to require is a planet that closely resembles your own—and planets are a dime a dozen, you know—and a sun of the proper type; and man, by one road or another, becomes disgustingly inevitable. One of man's attributes, by the way, is that until a certain rather low level of development, he always is quite certain that his own planet is the only fortunate one in the universe, being blessed with his presence."

Ellery downed his Scotch and puffed on his pipe. "Let's try another question, then," he said. "The gentlemen you sent for me mentioned saving me some time. I was given to understand you had some concrete proposal you were going to make to me. What were they talking about?"

John refilled both glasses and then got to his feet. He began pacing up and down behind his desk. Ellery got the distinct impression that the little fat man really had been enjoying their talk, just as he had enjoyed acting out the role of one of Frankenstein's afterthoughts when Ellery had first come in. Now, he was working again, and none too happy about it. Why?

"It's quite simple, Paul," he said, jamming his hands into

the pockets of his loose-fitting gray tunic. "You are, to put it candidly, an investigator who has been annoying our people. Now, suppose our positions were reversed. Suppose that you found an investigator who went around bothering *your* people—one without official immunity, let us say. What would you do with him?"

"Try to get rid of him, I suppose," Ellery said.

"Precisely. And how would you get rid of the investigator?"

"Well, you could lock him up if he had performed any criminal act. Or you could make things so hot for him he would have to go away and leave you alone. Or, failing all else, you might try to buy him off."

"Logical enough," John admitted, still pacing up and down. "Logical, but rather crude. I might almost say primitive—nothing personal, you understand."

"Naturally," said Ellery.

"Yes," said John. "We think we have a much more efficient method for getting unwanted investigators out of our hair."

"Which is?"

"Simplicity itself, old man. We simply take the problem that the investigator is trying to solve, and solve it for him! After that, we present him with the solution, with our compliments. Then, you see, the investigator finds himself in the untenable position of having nothing left to investigate. He has got the answers he was looking for and—presuming that he is an honest investigator—he can leave us in peace."

Ellery stared at the little man. "You mean you brought me up here to tell me what I've been trying to find out?"

"That's the general idea." John walked back to his desk and sat down. "There are things in the town of Jefferson

Springs which you do not understand and which bother you. You've seen ranchers come down out of the sky in a metal sphere, and you have seen this ship. You might think, incidentally, that Thorne was a bit careless in letting himself be spotted that way, but sometimes it *is* necessary to transport people back and forth. After all, it was done at night on Thorne's own ranch, and Thorne's land does not lie along a main road, you know. Even if it did, most people wouldn't spot that shadow in the sky. The few that might would be dismissed as flying-saucer addicts, and in any event we'd be gone before any lasting harm was done. Well! I'm going to tell you the works, Paul, the true story. After that, I'm going to make you an offer. Clear enough?"

"Clear so far."

"Okay," said John. "Here we go."

6

THE STORY THE fat man told was a strange mixture of the familiar and the unique. It was man—another race of man, perhaps, but man for all of that—writing the old, old stories on new paper with new machines.

There were many earthlike planets in the galaxy—rather small, unspectacular planets, orbited about quite ordinary suns. On every one, the alchemy of life had produced miracles in the seas, and the chain had begun. From the sea to the land, from reptile to amphibian to mammal; from simple to complex; from tiny, scuttling animal, sneaking a living from the domain of monsters, to man, proud and powerful and almost intelligent enough to be a long-term success instead of a flash in the pan.

The details were often different, but the generalized outline was the same. If you started with an Earthlike planet, you got an Earthlike man. Man was not quite an accident, and neither was he planned. He was the result of a set of conditions. Each group of men, when they arrived at a stage when they began to wonder about such things, naturally assumed that they were altogether too remarkable ever to be duplicated elsewhere in the known universe. Therefore, man's first inevitable contact with other men—for all men looked out at the stars, and all men wondered—always came as something of a shock.

People who had been living in villages found themselves also in a universe.

People who worried about nations discovered galaxies.

People who had learned to live in one world were dismayed to learn of a hundred thousand more.

Eventually, of course, great organizations and federations developed—man was an organizing animal. Planets which had reached a relatively high level of culture joined forces with other advanced planets. This was not easy, and took many centuries, for of course each planet felt that it had unique qualities; and it was difficult to trust foreigners. Each planet knew that it was superior and, what was more, each could prove it to its own satisfaction.

But civilization, which was another name for complexity and larger social aggregates, spread. At first, it was a few planets that had banded together, each for selfish purposes and each speaking loudly of brotherhood. Then it was many planets—for how could one lone planet survive against the power of many?

Man was an animal with big ideas.

The federation, loose and suspicious at first, thrived. Ideas were exchanged, and fresh viewpoints. Cultures flowered. A vast galactic government evolved, weak in the beginning, and then strong. Man could not live without organization.

When man on Earth was a clumsy thing climbing down from the trees, the first civilized planets were making overtures to each other.

When man on Earth found himself with a brain of sorts, and learned to make fire and pick up rocks with which to bash in other brains, a tenuous galactic federation was struggling to be born.

When man on Earth was yet a Neanderthal, slowly evolving the ideas of religion and an afterlife, other men he could not see had a civilization that spanned the known universe.

When man on Earth was a Cro-Magnon painting the walls of caves, he might look up at night, perhaps walking homeward from a mammoth hunt, and see the stars. Out there, a hundred thousand planets were jockeying for position on a galactic scale.

When man on Earth was an Indian, coming into an empty America across the Bering Strait from Asia, the star-civilization was running into difficulties.

When man on Earth was developing agriculture and cities and mushrooming technologies, the galactic troubles grew.

They had to be solved.

The interstellar civilization had thrived. When man thrives, he multiplies. The birth rate had gone up with the cultural vitality. Man filled up his planets, and the civilized planets of the galaxy became overcrowded.

The expanding population had to find some place to go. At first, non-human planets had been tried. Unfortunately, this had not worked out. The existing life-forms which occupied these other planets had been part of the trouble, but only a small part. For the most part, they were so utterly different that they had no interest in human beings one way or the other, and competition with them was out of the question—different life-forms lived different lives, and required different things.

The basic problem, however, was the planets themselves. If a planet was naturally suitable for human life, human life evolved there. If it wasn't naturally suitable, the mere question of survival for men posed tremendously difficult problems. It had been said many times that man was an extremely adaptable animal, and so he was—on his own planet, or on one closely resembling it. He didn't adapt very well to a planet with twenty gravities; he didn't exactly thrive on a methane atmosphere; he didn't find temperatures that melted rock very pleasant.

To be sure, there were some relatively unoccupied planets that man could exist on. He could build atmosphere domes and enclosed villages; he could substitute his technologies for nature. But only up to a point. Human populations didn't do well in plastic bowls. In some cases, they managed to stay alive, but they—changed.

Obviously, the "different" planets were no solution. Man needed Earthlike planets for his homes, because it had been Earthlike planets that had spawned him. On the right kind of a planet, on *his* kind of a planet, man worked. On other kinds, he didn't work, because he was a man. It was that simple.

The population continued to expand. The galactic civilization had to have Earthlike planets, had to have colonies that could drain off the overflow of men. Where could it find them?

There was only one place. If you want an Earthlike planet, a Marslike planet won't do. You can irrigate a desert and make it green, but you can't turn Jupiter into England with a slide rule. If you want an Earthlike planet, you must pick an Earthlike planet in the first place and go there.

It was unfortunate that *all* of the Earthlike planets were occupied.

It was more fortunate that all the Earthlike planets were not at the same level of cultural advancement. Many of them were quite primitive, others were just experiencing the growth pangs of civilizations.

Now, cultural simplicity has consequences over and beyond any moral condemnation or exaltation of the noble savage. It has consequences in terms of populations. A culture that exists by hunting and gathering, on the average, must be a small one. If the population of New York City alone had to live in New York State by hunting wild animals, it is a safe bet that the population would be drastically reduced. A culture that has farming can support more people on the available land surface. With the beginnings of machine technology, still more people can live on the same amount of land.

But it takes a galactic civilization *really* to fill up a planet. As a result, most of the Earthlike planets which had not yet become a part of the larger civilization still had some room left for expansion.

Earth was one of those planets.

The galactic civilization found itself in an odd position. On the one hand, it had developed to a point which made the ruthless conquering and exploiting of other worlds unthinkable. Its own citizens would never stand for such an action. On the other hand, it had to drain off population, and there were only the occupied Earthlike planets which offered any possibilities in that direction.

They did the best they could. Man, when forced into it,

is a compromising animal. They decided to colonize the undeveloped Earthlike planets left in the galaxy, but their colonization was no crude and slapdash affair. In order to appease public opinion within the federation, they had to work within a framework of principles, restrictions, and laws.

First of all, the primitive planet must not be aware that it had been colonized, for that would destroy initiative and rob whole worlds of their futures. Secondly, the natives could not be harmed in any way, and could not be interfered with except in the initial setting up of the colony, when various psychological techniques were permitted. Finally, there was a limit to the percentage of a planet that could be colonized. This percentage varied with the planet, but in no case could it exceed fifteen per cent.

Earth was one of the primitive planets selected.

There was nothing intentionally cruel about this idea, although it had its imperfections and unforeseen consequences. It was just an emergency solution to a pressing problem, and it postponed, at least, the necessity for long-term, sweeping reorganization and restriction. It was a practical program for thousands of years, in most cases, and as for the future—well, perhaps they would have other solutions then.

They were not *proud* of their solution, but they were stuck with it.

Ironically enough, there was a precise parallel on Earth itself, if on a more limited scale. On many parts of the planet, expanding Western civilization had reached out and enfolded more primitive cultures. In some cases, it had simply exterminated the natives. in others, it had just taken away their land and deposited the aborigines on reservations. It had happened quite strikingly in North America, among other places. The Europeans came in, and the Indians were presented with the short end of the stick.

We weren't a vicious people, the Europeans said afterward. *We weren't bloodthirsty fiends. But it was inevitable— all that land, supporting only a fraction of the people it could support. And we needed land, needed it badly. Perhaps we were wrong, in an abstract sense, but what happened couldn't be helped. No practical man could imagine leaving a whole continent to the Indians. We didn't always like it, but what else could we do?*

What, indeed?

And, argued the civilized peoples of the galaxy a few hundred years later, *what else could we do?*

When civilization came furtively to Earth, sneaking in by the back door as it were, it was all done with great finesse and subtlety. Advanced peoples employ advanced methods. There was no drum-thumping invasion, no excitement, no death rays, no battling space fleets. No one got hurt. The Earth never even knew it had company.

Planets had been colonized before. Methods were smooth and routine. No fuss, no muss, no bother.

Defense? How could there be a defense? Defense against what? Where was the offense?

Naturally, the colonists confined themselves to the small towns and villages. They had other uses for the cities.

Picture a small town, any small town. A Main Street and a drugstore and a movie. Houses with unpainted, honest fronts and hamburgers cooking in the kitchen. Snow in the winter, sun in the summer. Rain on the night of the big dance. Rotary Clubs and gas stations. Gray ladies worried about the new preacher—he smokes, you know. A boy and a girl on a night in spring, the family car kissed by magic, a soft moon forgotten among the stars.

The town, though caught in the web of nation and state, is isolated. The people there see the same people every day. The next town is twenty miles away, and of course the people in the next town are hardly the *proper* sort. Strangers aren't wanted, because strangers always want to change things. We like our town the way it is.

The small town has a reputation in the city. The people who live and die there are ignorant, so the legend goes. They are fifty years behind the times. You can't ever tell about small towns—they're funny. They're full of local color and strange rural customs and the damnedest characters you ever saw.

An isolated society, then. A clannish society that doesn't want strangers poking around. A backward society where odd things and unusual-looking people are a part of life. Buildings all up, crops all planted, stores all stocked. A rustic colony. Ideal conditions. Ready for immediate occupancy.

The scientific experts from an unsuspected civilization go to work. Buy here, sell there. Tamper with a crop here, dust a few cattle there. Alter the rainfall, just a little. Spread a few pointed stories around—why, they're cleaning up down the road in Oakville, or out in Indiana, or right over there in the city. Opportunity!

And new people move into your little town. Funny people. They don't mix. Why, they're taking over the town, I declare! It's all poor Mrs. Smith can do to keep body and soul together. And so many of your friends moving on, after all these years, selling out, going to the city.

It's just not the same in your town any more. And you've

heard of such wonderful chances somewhere else—the Wilsons went there, remember, and the Wades and the Flahertys——

Will, I've been wondering——

It was a snap. Duck soup for the experts from the stars. One population moved out, another population moved in.

A colony.

Of course, it was unfortunately true that if you moved the natives off their land you had to be sure they had somewhere to go. Fifteen per cent of a planet was a lot of real estate. There had to be, in a sense, reservations for the natives.

Earth was ideal. Earth already had its reservations, ready and waiting. They were called cities.

Where did the unabsorbed small-town people go when they left home? Where had they always gone? Into the cities, of course.

The cities of Earth became preserves for the aborigines.

It was beautiful, really. What sane man would prefer to live in the shrieking chaos of a city, stacked in like sardines with his neighbors in the smoke and the dirt and the sweat? What sane man would voluntarily leave the sunshine and the green fields and the quiet companionship of home for a factory and a tenement and the grinding of machinery?

Answer: almost all of them. Wasn't it the thing to do? Wasn't the city the place to go to get ahead? Wasn't the city where all the smart people were? Weren't you an ignorant hick if you stayed at home?

There was nothing new in this. Man had always gone to the city. But he could be helped along if necessary, and he was. Psychological conditioning techniques, when administered by a really advanced culture, were remarkable things.

If you want to build an escape-proof prison, there is a way. Just don't tell the prisoners that they're in jail. Make them compete with each other for life-sentences.

Call it home.

There was one colossal irony in what was happening on the Earth, and it afforded the colonists with no end of amusement. The technicians of Earth were busily engaged in trying to build a spaceship of their own—one of the first primitive types, of course, with chemical fuels. With this spaceship of theirs, if it ever got off the drawing boards, they hoped to transport colonies of *natives* to other planets! They were bravely hoping one day to go out and "conquer" and populate the galaxy—a galaxy that was already so overcrowded that it had overflowed to Earth!

Naturally, they would find that the other planets of their solar system were quite unsuited for colonies of any sort, and they were still many centuries away from a workable interstellar drive. Still, it was amusing.

Since Earth was now entering a primitive phase of what might be termed pre-civilization, with savage war patterns coupled with semi-advanced destructive techniques, it might well be that an atomic war could occur. Earth was at a crisis period in her history, and could easily go either forward or backward. Many of the Earthlike planets had reached this stage many times, only to be blown back to the beginning for another start. Some planets never did get any further.

Now, an atomic war, under present conditions, would primarily affect only the large cities. This was not a pleasant prospect, of course, but for the colonists it was far from being a tragedy. The longer it took Earth to evolve a true civilization, the more time the colonies had to live their lives undisturbed.

Mind you, they would not start the war. They were not immoral beasts. Starting a war would be very unethical. On the other hand, they were forbidden to interfere. They just wouldn't *prevent* the war. Savages were so warlike.

The town of Jefferson Springs, obviously, was one of the alien colonies. It went through the typical well-trained motions of an American village, but this was no village of Earth.

This was different.

And that was the story the fat man told.

7

THERE WAS A brief silence while John paused for breath. He occupied himself by refilling the neglected glasses with Scotch and indulging in another cigarette. He looked just faintly bored—the look of a college professor explaining evolution to a freshman.

"Well, that's that," he said. "I hope I haven't bored you?"

"Not at all," said Paul Ellery. *When all else is gone*, he told himself, *put up a good front.*

"No monsters, no fiends, no wicked prime ministers," the fat little man observed, rather sadly. "Not even much drama, I'm afraid, to say nothing of melodrama. Just expediency. Just politics. Just human littleness in the face of something big." He sipped his drink. "I sometimes think that men are too small for their universe, Paul. We have such a magnificent backdrop, and our plays are so confoundedly uninspired and monotonous."

"Yeah," said Paul Ellery. "Monotonous."

"I'm quite serious," John said. "You will find that life on a galactic scale can be every bit as humdrum as life confined to a planetary anthill. Sam still loves Mary, and Mary still wants Sam to be a bigger wheel than Philip. It's all damnably dull if you ask me, which you didn't."

Paul Ellery, Ph.D., born in Austin, Texas, and raised on the planet Earth, puffed on his pipe in a spaceship room, hanging in the night. It was his fourth pipe, and his mouth felt like sandpaper. The rest of him felt worse.

He felt numb with what he had heard. It was not so much that it had come as a complete surprise, for much of his information had pointed the same way. Rather, it was the fact that his wildest conjectures, his most fantastic guesses, had been reduced to the level of a commonplace, everyday existence.

Little green men living in your furnace? Why, of course! Didn't you know?

John's matter-of-fact attitude toward the whole thing had made him feel oddly distant from the whole problem. It was like an intellectual exercise, a bedtime story in bedlam, a motion picture about another world.

It wasn't easy to remember that *he* was an aborigine. Ph.D.? He had never been unduly proud of it, but it *was* disconcerting to have it calmly reduced to the level of Witch Doctor, Third Class. *Some of his herbs really work, you know, but all that mumbo-jumbo is just too much for me.*

He couldn't doubt the story he had heard. It fitted the evidence too well, and the quiet ship that surrounded him squelched any qualms he might have had with complete authority. There was no reason for John to lie to him. He had heard the truth and he knew it.

He had one question, however.

"Look, John," he said slowly. "You kept talking about the inevitability of these colonies. You kept speaking of the necessity for what you did, and you used some examples from our own history to justify your viewpoint. But isn't there a basic difference? After all, this outfit of yours is a galactic civilization. It's big business. Wouldn't birth control have solved your whole population problem very neatly?"

John smiled. "No, it wouldn't," he said.

"Why? Surely your people are sophisticated enough——"

"That's not the point, Paul. Look here—you have birth control available and widely practiced right in the United States, isn't that right? And has the population gone up or down since the introduction of birth control techniques?"

"Up," Ellery had to admit. "But I still think——"

"No, my friend. It isn't that simple. Many other factors are involved. For one thing, the galactic federation is not a dictatorial set-up—and it takes a dictatorship to impose that sort of a rigid restriction on people. You will find that as people advance they insist on a certain amount of individual freedom; they will submit voluntarily to some things, but not to others. Birth control is practiced to some extent, just as it is in the United States, and you will observe that the birth rate in Jefferson Springs is actually lower than in most American towns. That isn't enough, however—it's a phony solution."

"Why?"

"You know the answer to that one, Paul. Permit me to refer you to one of your own scientists, V. Gordon Childe. What has *always* happened when there is a technological advance? What happened in the Neolithic? What happened during the Industrial Revolution?"

Ellery saw the point. "The population expands," he admitted.

"Check. And you are *sitting* right smack in the middle of a technological advance—a spaceship. Spaceflight *always* means more population, not less. That's just the way it is. If there's a method of cutting down population without killing the culture, we haven't found it yet. It's a problem for the future. We don't know all the answers, Paul, and we never will."

Ellery let that sink in a minute. There was just one thing he could say. He said it. "You spoke of an offer, John."

John put the tips of his fingers together and twiddled his thumbs. "Paul, you're an intelligent man. The fact that I am from what we have modestly described as a high civilization and you are a citizen of, shall we say, a less developed culture, has no bearing on your *intelligence*. We respect your brains. We know our own self-interest when we see it, and we think we could find a place for you in Jefferson Springs. Not much of a place at first, to be candid, but with hope for the future. We want you to work for us. That way, we gain and you gain. The other way, nobody gains. You have a saying on your planet, I believe, one of the few that makes a modicum of sense: If you can't beat 'em, join 'em. Crude, but I'm sure you see the point."

Ellery looked at the fat little man—the friendly blue eyes, the lines in the pink forehead, the earnestness that filtered through the easy mannerisms. Whatever else he was, John was an intelligent man. More to the point, he seemed to be an honest man. "Suppose I don't accept your offer?"

"You are indeed a suspicious man," John sighed. "I'm afraid you still think of me as a monster of some sort."

"Not a monster, John," Ellery said truthfully. "I'm trying to deal with you as a human being."

"What is there to say, my friend? If you don't accept our offer, you don't accept our offer. That's all. Nothing will happen to you—although the psychological effects are apt to

be rather overpowering. You are free to leave here, go anywhere you want to go, say anything you want to say. We think
you have a brain, and we hope you use it. It's up to you."

Ellery hesitated. "You mean I am actually free to leave,
after what you've told me?"

John nodded at the door. "There's the exit. You will be
escorted back to your room, unconditioned and unin-
fluenced. You're a free agent—or as much of one as a human
being ever is. You know Mel Thorne. If you want to take us
up on our offer, go out and see him. If not, I wish you well."

Paul Ellery got to his feet, slowly.

"So long, Paul," John said, shaking his hand firmly.

"So long—and thanks. I appreciate—well, everything."

"It was a pleasure, my friend." John looked as though he
meant it.

The big door opened silently for him. He left the fat man
alone at his desk. He seemed a little lonely, a little sad. The
two escorts were waiting in the long, cool corridor.

Ellery followed them down the timeless, deserted tunnel, past the side panels that lined the walls. There was the
door, the short passage, another door—and he was back in the
sphere. He sat down on the green couch on the gray carpet,
and the humming vibration came again.

When the sliding panel opened again, he emerged into
the moist coolness of false dawn. He heard crickets chirping
in the damp grass. He looked at his watch. It was five o'clock
in the morning. There was the ride in the Buick, hardly
remembered, and then he was back in his hotel room. His
two guides left, and he was alone.

He sat down on the edge of the bed, in the darkness. He
felt terrible. Too much Scotch, too much tobacco, too much
everything. At long last, a hollow reaction caught up with

him. He had left one world a short two months ago, his life secure and his future comfortable. He had come back to a new world this morning. His future might be—anything.

He got up, pulled the .38 from his belt, and stuck it back in the dresser drawer. Then he fell down on the bed, clothes and all, and stared at the gray light of morning until he fell into a light and fitful sleep.

He twisted and turned as the hours passed and the blistering heat came again. Twice, he cried out.

He woke up shortly after noon; it was too hot to sleep any more, and his pillow was wet with sweat. He managed to shave and take a cold shower in the bathroom at the end of the hall, and when he had put on fresh clothes he felt a little better.

He didn't even try to think until after he had downed four cups of black coffee at the cafe, and managed to choke down two overdone eggs and some passable sausage. Then he got into his car, opened all the windows, and just drove. He wasn't going anywhere, he just wanted the air to circulate a little. The sun was like a big brass shield in an absolutely empty sky.

He thought, briefly, of going to Austin, but he couldn't quite face it. He had dimly hoped that when he woke up, despite John's assurances, he wouldn't remember a thing that had happened the night before. But he remembered it.

All of it.

He simply couldn't go into the city yet.

He recognized, with painful clarity, the utter hopelessness of his position. Things weren't the same any more, and they would never be the same again, not for him.

Sure, he had the whole story now—or most of it. There was no more problem. He had the answer he had sought.

Great.

Fabulous.

What could he do with it? *Nothing.* Absolutely nothing. He thought of every conceivable angle. He analyzed every possible course of action. He planned at least fifty different moves, and promptly discarded every one of them.

It was impossible for him, being what he was, just to put Jefferson Springs and all that it meant out of his mind, leave the place for good, and try to find any meaning in the life he would have to lead. It was a shock, to put it mildly, to find out that he was a primitive, a savage, sitting in his little village and calmly assuming that he was king of all he surveyed. A man—or at least Ellery's kind of man—couldn't go on with his work, knowing that all he was working for was thousands of years old-hat to a civilization of which he could never be a part. He couldn't face his friends every day, working, laughing, dreaming their dreams—when all the time he knew.

He would look up at the stars at night, and one night he would pull the trigger.

He could not write up what he had discovered in a technical paper. The idea was laughable. *Some Evidence Pertaining to an Alien Colony in Texas, with Suggestions about a Galactic Civilization.* No reputable journal would touch such an article for a million dollars. And if it were published, what difference would it make? Who would believe it? Even if the world's most famous scientist seriously advanced such a theory, he would be quietly carted off to an insane asylum.

And Paul Ellery was not the world's most famous scientist. There were several hundred thousand or so ahead of him.

He could not go to the newspapers or to the police. What

could he say? He could hear himself: "Look, do you know the town of Jefferson Springs? It's been taken over by aliens, people from out of space. That's right, *space*. You know. You see, they took me into their spaceship one night and told me the whole story. It's like this . . ."

He couldn't even tell his best friend. "Look, Joe, a funny thing happened to me while I was working in Jefferson Springs. I know this sounds nuts, but . . ."

It was hopeless.

It was hopeless precisely because the colonists really *were* far more advanced than the cultures of Earth. The whole problem that the colony posed, a problem in philosophy and psychology and ethics as well as in survival, was virtually inconceivable as a serious situation to a planet at Earth's development stage. It was precisely analogous to a Neanderthal shouting into his cave that he had just split the atom.

Hopeless, too, because there *was* no Earth. There were only the hostile nations, glaring at each other in armed truce. There was only the U.N., fighting to be born in a world that needed it desperately but wasn't ready for it yet.

Could you address the United States Senate and suggest that aliens from outer space made up many of the senators' constituents? Ellery didn't even want to think about that possibility.

A revolution as an answer was sophomoric. Who would revolt? Against what? The plain fact was that Earth had evolved no technique even faintly suitable to handling the situation. It was outside Earth's experience, outside her expectations. It was even worse than trying to stop a tank with a bow and arrow. Earth could not even recognize that the tank *existed*.

There was only one thing he could do, obviously. There

was no answer to the new problem that had been created by the solution to the old problem. All right, accept that. Therefore, his job was easily stated: *find one.*

He actually knew little or nothing about what really went on in the town of Jefferson Springs. He knew the familiar patterns designed for public consumption, and he knew at least something of the true story behind the colony. Beyond that, he was ignorant. The inner life of the colony, the genuine, functioning community culture—all that was unknown.

What was the actual relationship of the colony to Earth? Was it at worst a harmless parasite, as John had suggested? Or were these people human enough to want their colony to continue for always? Would the colonists *really* leave Earth alone to work out its own affairs? How could they be controlled that closely?

And how did the damned thing *work?* How could people, real people, live out their lives in a masquerade, pretending to be virtual savages from their point of view? Roughing it was fine for a vacation, even for a year or two. But for a lifetime?

Paul Ellery thought about Jefferson Springs—the real Jefferson Springs that he had never penetrated. Possibly—just possibly—there was a clue there. If he could find it.

He didn't really think he could. It was a needle in a haystack, at best. He wasn't even sure what it was he would have to look for. It was a million-to-one shot. But Paul Ellery was a stubborn man. He was also a practical man. He repeated the words to himself: *If you can't beat 'em, join 'em.*

He told himself that he was motivated by pure self-interest. He told himself that he was too sensible to try to save the world. Saving the world was a large order, with or without colonists from the stars. The hydrogen bomb was a tough opponent in a debate.

If he could come up with no solution, he would just have to make the best of things. He would have to adjust. He had been given a chance. Many a native before him had had to leave his tribe and try to learn the strange ways of civilization. He remembered his friend Two Bears, his interpreter among the Hawks. Two Bears was one of many Indians he had known, caught between two opposing lifeways. What were they called in the literature?

Marginal men.

He would try to find a flaw in the colony's armor. He would do the best he could. That was all he could do.

It was evening when he turned his Ford around and drove back to Jefferson Springs. The long shadows lay like soft fingers across the fields and the brush and the cactus. The faint breeze was only another shadow, whispering over the clean, sweet land. Jefferson Springs baked in the late sun, one hundred and twenty miles from San Antonio, sixty miles from the Rio Grande and Mexico.

Paul Ellery had made up his mind.

He had become a hired man. Not a *hired* man, he reminded himself, but a hired *man*. There was a difference.

Tomorrow, he would drive out again to see Melvin Thorne.

8

THE NEXT DAY was like all the rest. The burning sun was up early, sucking the night moisture out of the air, and again turning Paul Ellery's hotel room in the Rocking-T into a boxlike oven. It was wrong, somehow, that the day should still be the same. So much had happened, so much had changed, that the most incredible thing of all, the most difficult fact to accept, was that the world went on, inevitable and unimpressed.

Ellery ate a perfectly ordinary breakfast—no worse than usual—and was faintly surprised to find that he had a good appetite. In fact, he felt fine. The pressure was off, and if what was left was mainly resignation—well, that was still an improvement.

He went back to his hotel room, took off his shirt, and propped himself up on the bed, using a bulky copy of *Anthropology Today* as a writing desk. His handwriting was none too beautiful, but his typing was worse.

He had three letters to write.

The first was to Winans University. Winans was a small, privately endowed school, a few miles north of Austin, near

Round Rock. It had been established thirty years ago by old
Edgar V. Winans, an eccentric Texas millionaire who had,
surprisingly, graduated from Harvard. Winans had failed to
see why his native state could not support a really *good* small
college, and to prove his point he had built Winans University. Winans was a man who knew what he was doing, and
when he was through he had a first-class school on his hands,
and one that attracted high-caliber students. Ellery, who had
been teaching at the University of Texas, had resigned before
coming to Jefferson Springs on the Norse grant. He had an
offer from Winans University, which he had tentatively accepted because he liked small schools and the pay was good.

That, of course, had been in the other world.

Now, he dropped a note to Bud Winans, the old gentleman's capable son, and told him that he couldn't make it by
September. He said that his plans were indefinite for a while,
but that he would give him a definite answer as soon as he
could. Hardly standard operating procedure, but Bud was a
good guy, and would pull the necessary strings.

The second letter was to his parents. This was a more
conventional item, hinting broadly at hard work and unexpected complications, and said in effect that he would be very
busy for a while, but would try to see them soon.

The third letter was to Anne. This one required more
skill. He had to prevent her from getting lonesome and
coming to see him; and on the other hand he had to keep in
her good graces in case he should decide to see *her*. This
wasn't too difficult, being a type of letter that all young men
learn to write to their girls, although Ellery had a sneaking
suspicion that Anne was never fooled a bit.

He thought of Anne, only a short distance away in
Austin, and felt a strong desire to go to her, be with her. But

he rejected the idea almost before it was born. Nice, yes—but the answer to *his* problem wasn't in Austin.

He took his camera off the dresser and loaded it. It was a most unspectacular box Brownie. Ellery wasn't certain what he intended to do with it, but he figured that a few pictures here and there wouldn't hurt anything.

He dropped the letters in the slot at the ramshackle post office, across the street near the Rialto. Now showing at the Rialto: *Rocketship X-M.* Ellery guessed that *that* one would be well attended. Coincidence—or did all the colonists have an odd sense of humor?

He got into his Ford, stopped and bought gas at the Humble station, and tried to tell himself that the station attendant was an alien colonist. It didn't work. The overalls, the clumsy shoes, the red bandanna hanging out of a back pocket—the man was just too damned *ordinary*.

He had to keep telling himself: *This is not real, this is an alien colony, this is not real*——

The words were not real, either.

He drove off, back out of town and out across the Nueces bridge to the Thorne Ranch. He did his best to choke off both his mood and his train of thought. The treadmill thinking that kept rolling off *this-can't-be-real-but-it-is-real-but-it-doesn't-LOOK-real* wasn't helping a bit. He had to keep his mind clear.

For himself, of course. He came first.

He drove along through the familiar country, along the familiar gravel road, and turned off at the dirt road that led to the ranch house. He looked up, half expecting to see a great ship swimming in the air, but the pale blue sky was empty. There was only the sun, relentlessly pressing the attack.

He pulled into the ranch driveway and parked. No pictures yet, he decided. He got out and knocked on the door. He heard footsteps, but they were not those of Thorne's clumping boots. His wife, maybe?

The door opened. It wasn't his wife.

"Hello," said the girl, smiling. "Are you Paul Ellery?"

"I used to be," Ellery said.

"Please come in, Paul. I'm Cynthia. I'll call Mel."

Ellery followed her into the house, caught off base again. The girl was a surprise. She was a blonde, with her hair piled up on top of her head, careless of her looks because she had them to spare. She wore a man's white shirt with the sleeves rolled up, and gray shorts. Her feet were bare.

"Sit down, Paul," she said.

Ellery sat down. He was in the living room this time, on a brown couch. The big clock ticked monotonously in the heat.

"Mel's out in the barn," Cynthia said. Her voice was soft, but it had a definite Texas slur in it. "Don't go 'way."

She left, and Ellery heard her call. She had a good pair of lungs, among other things. Ellery tried to add her into the equation. Mistress? New colonist from the ship? Bait? Friend of the family? Vampire?

Cynthia came back. "My God, it's hot here," she said.

That, Ellery reflected, was a statement with at least two hidden jokes in it. Who or what her God might be, he had not the foggiest notion. And the way she said "here" suggested strongly that she had just arrived from elsewhere. However, if nothing else, the sentence neatly destroyed the picture of her as a *femme fatale* he had been building up in his mind.

"It is hot," he said wittily. Then, ashamed of himself, he

tried to do better. "Do you live here?" Not much of an improvement.

"Yes," she said, sitting down next to him on the couch. "In town," she added. "I teach home economics in the high school."

Ellery let that digest a minute, and discovered that her eyes were the standard blue. Age? Early twenties, probably.

"That's nice," he said. "For the students, I mean."

She smiled. "Thank you, Paul," she said demurely.

The back door slammed and there were more footsteps. Clumping ones, this time. Melvin Thorne walked into the room, big and solid and sweating. He held his hat in his hand, and he was wearing tight, faded blue jeans and a dirty khaki shirt. The cowboy boots were scuffed.

"Howdy, Paul," he drawled. "Mighty glad to see you again."

Oh no, thought Ellery a little wildly. *Not the dialect again.*

"Hello, Mel. How are you?"

"Fine, mighty fine." The big man paused. "Cynthia, you get the hell out of here." He said it in exactly the tone of voice he would have used to say, "Cynthia, please pour me another cup of coffee."

Cynthia raised her neat eyebrows but made no objection. She stood up, looking very cool and slim next to Thorne. "See you later, Paul," she said, and left the room.

"You want to watch out for that one, son," Melvin Thorne said. "She's trouble. Come on into the kitchen where we can talk."

They went back into the kitchen and sat down at the battered wood table with the red-and-white checked tablecloth. The salt and pepper shakers still carried their inane legends, unashamed. Before Thorne had a chance to say anything, his wife padded into the kitchen. She was dumpy, white-haired, scrubbed. She had nice brown eyes.

"Pour us some coffee, Martha," Melvin Thorne said.

Martha obliged, pouring from the big black pot on the stove into two mugs that had seen better days. She didn't bother about sugar or cream. She eyed Ellery for a moment, and then put a strong hand on his shoulder.

"You'll be Mr. Ellery," she said. "You look like a nice young man, and I hope you like it here with us."

"Thank you, Mrs. Thorne," Ellery said. "Thanks a lot."

Again, he looked at Mr. and Mrs. Melvin Thorne. Could these people really be "alien," and what did that mean? If they had evolved on a planet that circled another sun, was that so horrible? What was the difference?

Why is there a threat to Earth at all? A threat to me? Why shouldn't they live here, the same as anybody else?

But he remembered, even there in that cozy kitchen. He remembered all those primitive peoples who had come face to face with the white man. The white man had evolved on the same planet they had, and was indistinguishable from them except for a few minor traits. Where were those primitive peoples now? These aliens, or whatever they were, said that they had no desire to "conquer" the Earth. As far as Ellery could tell, that was true. But more of them were coming all the time, looking for living space. They were not machines. They had their weaknesses the same as other people.

Some day, that meant trouble.

Paul Ellery wondered: *Had any colonized planet ever*

climbed out of savagery? Or were they—helped—to stay where they were?

He thought, too, of the hydrogen bombs and all that they represented. The civilized aliens could prevent those bombs from ever going off, could wipe war from the Earth forever. But they wouldn't. Here, if anywhere, they would not interfere. What chance did Earth have, on its own?

Paul Ellery clenched his fists. Well, here was one way out—for him.

"I guess John told you the story," he said.

"I heard from old John, that's right," Melvin Thorne said, drinking his coffee. "Reckon you've decided to tie up with us, that right?"

"That's right," Ellery said. He swallowed his coffee more out of politeness than desire. Gulping hot coffee in the middle of the day in summer was one Texas custom he had never made his own. "He told me you'd tell me what I needed to know."

"Mighty glad to help, Paul," Thorne said slowly. "Though there ain't an all-fired lot to tell."

Melvin Thorne was still employing his Texas drawl, and Ellery suddenly realized that it wasn't faked at all. *This was the only English the man knew.* He had been trained for this particular culture—for how long? Ellery began to appreciate something of the stake that Thorne and the rest had in staying in Jefferson Springs. Where else could they go?

"It will have to be sort of odd jobs at first, Paul, until we're sure and you're sure that you want to stay on with us," Mel said, pouring more coffee. "You understand, I reckon, that it will take you a spell to fit into the *real* life of our town. You've got a lot to learn, just like I had a lot to learn before I came down here and set me up a ranch. I think the paper would be a good place for you to start, since you like readin' and all that stuff anyhow. We'll keep you at that a spell, and then give you a shot at something else. It won't be very exciting at first, Paul, but we think we've got a nice little town here and we're proud of it."

Ellery listened in growing wonderment. Thorne was just the same as he had been before—evidently he really *was* more or less what he appeared to be on the surface. Personality type screening? Right man for the right job? Somehow, he hadn't expected an alien from an advanced civilization to be of no better than average intelligence. But why not? It was the civilization that was advanced, not the citizen. The fact that Joe Blow lives in the same culture as Albert Einstein does not mean that Joe Blow can't be a Grade-Q moron. And Mel Thorne seemed to be—what? A Texas Babbitt from another planet? It was a vaguely frightening thought.

"I'll do my best, Mel," he said.

"I'm sure you will, son. And later on, if you get along okay, they may send you—back—for the full treatment."

"Back?"

"That's right—back. You know. But for right now it'll have to be the newspaper."

"Well," Ellery said, "it could be worse. They used to have a standard joke in college that all the guys with a Ph.D. wound up digging ditches."

Melvin Thorne laughed—a big, booming, noisy laugh. "That's a good one, son," he said. "I always said that there book learnin' was a waste of time."

Ellery sighed. The man *meant* it. It was no act. "Well, I'll try to rise above it," he said.

Mrs. Thorne came back into the kitchen, smiled vacantly, and padded out again.

"One thing we *can* do for you right at the start," Mel told him, "and that's get you out of that Rocking-T hotel. That place is just to scare the tourists off."

He laughed. Ellery laughed with him, unamused.

"You just go on into that little white house across from the high school," Thorne said. "Ain't nobody living there, so that's your house now. You'll find the key in the mailbox."

"Thanks again," Ellery said. His mind set up a pleasant equation: house plus high school equals Cynthia.

"And keep an eye out for Cynthia, son," Thorne said. "She's trouble, like I said. She teaches high school, you know."

"I know," Ellery said. "I'll wear my armor."

"Uh huh," Thorne said doubtfully. "Well, that's about it, Paul. I want you to feel free to come out here and see me any old time. And remember this, son: you're not a prisoner here. This is your *home*, if you want it. You're free to leave whenever you want to. We're right proud of what we've done in Jefferson Springs; we've worked hard for what we've got. Just remember, it ain't half as funny to you as it was to us when we first came here.'

Ellery caught just a glimpse then of Jefferson Springs the way the colonists saw it. An alien town on a strange and distant world, a tiny spot torn out of a hostile wilderness, a fragile container into which they poured their lives and their loves and their hopes. An adventure on another world, as surely as though it had been men from Earth journeying to the stars. . . .

"Thanks, Mel," he said.

"Don't mention it, son."

Paul Ellery went back through the living room and out the door. He didn't see Cynthia. He gunned his Ford down the dirt road. The brilliant sunshine touched the blue sky with gold, and the heat was heavy with the rich smell of the river and the cypress trees.

He breathed deeply of summer and tried not to think.

9

H IS FIRST DAY on the weeky newspaper was singular enough for any man.

The *Watchguard* office, located across from the Community Hall, was a long, narrow, and magnificely drab shed. It was so palpably ancient that Ellery half expected to find that all the writing was done by hooded scribes with goose-quill pens.

Instead, it was done by Abner Jeremiah Stubbs.

Mr. Stubbs was tall, stooped, and thin. He was pleasantly grotesque. His hair was a precise nothing-color, and it was kept out of his eyes by a faded green eye shade. He dressed in a black suit. His shapeless coat was hung on a hook on the door, and he worked in a shiny vest. He had a big gold watch, and Ellery knew without checking that it was scrupulously accurate.

Abner spoke in funereal tones, when he spoke at all. Everything he said came out sounding like, "Ah, the pity of it all, the *vast* pity of it all."

To Ellery, he said: "Typewriter's in the next room. Telephone's there too. List of stories on the pad. You know make-up?"

"Only the kind that goes on girls' faces," Ellery confided.

Mr. Stubbs nodded wearily. Another day, another burden. "You'll learn. Get ink in your blood."

Ellery nodded. Mr. Stubbs leaned back in his swivel chair and gazed blankly at the wall, so Ellery decided that the interview was over. He went into his office, if it could be dignified by that name, and risked the wrath of ageless gods by wrestling up a window that acted as if it had been shut since the Flood. The Flood hadn't washed it any too clean, either.

The heat was stifling. Outside the window, a single forlorn oak tree drooped in the sun and tried to remember what rain looked like. Ellery sat at a small, unpainted table and contemplated a typewriter that must have been older than he was.

He had, of course, studied the paper intensively in his work in Jefferson Springs. Every item in it for months before he had arrived in the town had been classified and filed. The news items had given him information on kinship connections, meetings, parties. They had furnished valuable interview leads. The editorials of Mr. Stubbs had yielded insights into the value system of Jefferson Springs.

Ellery knew the paper. He had never been much of a writer, but he felt supremely confident that he could attain the required stylistic excellence. The paper was called *The Jefferson Springs Watchguard*. Its slogan: OUR FIGHT FOR THE RIGHT IS ETERNAL AS THE PLAINS.

Not much of a slogan, he reflected, but better than some he had seen. There was one town in East Texas with a paper called the *Jimplecute: Join Industry, Manufacturing, Planting, Labor, Energy, Capital (in) Unity Together Everlasting.*

He studied the scrawled pad for thirty minutes and then stuck a yellow sheet in the typewriter. In three hours he wrote four stories, and between the battered typewriter and his own unskilled fingers he managed to produce a mess worthy of any seasoned reporter. Casting inexperience to the winds, he composed four headlines to go with the stories. He was happily ignorant of word-counts and allied trivia, but he caught the tone of the *Watchguard* to perfection:

MILDEW IS COMMON PROBLEM OF SUMMER.
LITTLE JODY DAVIS IMPROVED AFTER BEING KICKED IN FACE BY HORSE.
A 4-H CAMPER WRITES HOME TO MOM.
LIONS CLUB BANQUET IS VERY ENJOYABLE EVENT.

His day's work done, Ellery examined the last issue of the paper, trying to find something in it that would prove useful to him. Here again was the basic anomaly of Jefferson Springs. The town was an alien colony but there was nothing advanced about it that he could see. It was as average as dirt. Now, acting or no acting, false-face or not, the colonists actually *were* living in Jefferson Springs. No matter how insincere—and it did not strike Ellery that they were insincere at all in the lives they led—the mere business of going through the motions of life in Jefferson Springs took time, a lot of time. These people spent, without any doubt, the majority of their lives acting out the parts of small-town Texas citizens.

And that didn't make sense.

These colonists were human enough, as far as Ellery could tell. No group of people would willingly spend at least seventy per cent of every single day pretending to live in a culture without meaning for them.

Ellery reversed a few positions in order to see the problem more clearly. Suppose that the cultures concerned were those of the present-day United States and a Southeastern Indian group, say the Natchez who had once lived on the lower Mississippi. The gulf between the two cultures was roughly comparable to the gulf between a galactic civilization and the United States, though possibly not as profound. Okay, that was the setup. On one hand, modern industrialized America. On the other, seven villages of thatched huts, agricultural, with temple mounds and undying-fire ceremonies, together with a well-defined class system ranging from a supreme Sun down through Nobles, Honored Men, and commoners, the last known as Stinkards. Now, suppose that for some reason the present-day Americans wish to set up a colony among the Natchez, and do it in such a way that the Natchez are unaware of the colony's presence. First, of course, there would have to be an intensive period of detailed training, to say nothing of time travel. But, assuming that the United States citizens could turn themselves into a reasonable facsimile of Natchez Indians, how long would they be willing to *live* like the Indians, cut off from all the comforts and conveniences and values of the life they had known? Not for a week or so, not for a summer's outing, but for *keeps*?

Ellery could see only one possibility there: if the United States citizens were taken as children and brought up as Indians, then they would, of course, be perfectly content with the Indian culture, since they would, in effect, *be* Indians. They would not, however, be typical United States citizens any longer.

That was the possibility. It was unfortunate that the aliens weren't working it that way.

Quite clearly, it wouldn't work in their case. Their problem was considerably more complex. They must both fit their citizens for life in a primitive colony and at the same time retain them as participants in a galactic civilization. Simply dumping them down in Jefferson Springs as children wouldn't do the trick, and in any event he had already seen enough to indicate that the procedure was quite different. Some of the colonists came to Jefferson Springs as young adults; that called for one technique. Some of them came as children; that meant another technique. And some, apparently, were born in Jefferson Springs and then trained as full galactic citizens elsewhere.

Sent "back for the full treatment," as Thorne had intimated that Ellery would be eventually?

The question remained: how could they be both? How could they live in and *enjoy*— for they must enjoy it—Jefferson Springs, and at the same time maintain their unity with a vast and complex interstellar civilization?

Ellery had no answer for that one.

He read the paper carefully, digesting every last "personal" ("Mr. and Mrs. Joe Walker spent two happy days last week visiting in Garner State Park") and advertisement ("Mr. Merchant: Don't Preach Home Patronage then Send Your Printing Elsewhere"). In the entire paper, he found only one small item that was at all suggestive. It was suggestive only because it was cryptic; there was nothing blatantly mysterious about it. It was a small square on the back page:

THORNE RANCH
COMPULSORY
AUGUST 25   9 P.M.

That was all. And the date was the day after tomorrow. Paul Ellery didn't know what it was, or even what it might be.

He did know that he was going to be there.

He walked out of his office and handed his completed stories to Mr. Stubbs, who was still seated in his swivel chair gazing with complete absorption at the wall. Stubbs fished out his gold watch, shook his head sadly, and said nothing.

Ellery chose to interpret this as both approval and dismissal, and left for the day. He drove home to his new white house across from the high school, which was deserted for the summer. The house was just beginning to cool off from the afternoon roasting, but it was still plenty warm. There was a slight breeze out of the north, but Ellery had no instruments delicate enough to detect it.

The house was plain but comfortable: living room, bathroom, bedroom, kitchen, a few closets, all put together without a single trace of either ingenuity or imagination. There was one painting in the place, a waxen floral study, and when it had been carefully turned to face the wall it was passable.

Ellery fried himself a hamburger, preferring even his own cooking to that of the Jefferson Springs Cafe, and opened a bottle of beer. He armed himself with a notebook and a pencil and sat down at the kitchen table.

He asked himself what he, as an anthropologist, knew about the problems of culture contact that would be useful to him. He was not given to getting in over his head and asking questions afterward; he had found that it was to his advantage to figure things out ahead of time. If he could.

When the knock on the door came, he was halfway through the hamburger. On the problems of culture contact, his progress was less remarkable. He stuck the notebook in a drawer in the kitchen table and opened the front door.

It was Cynthia. The equation ran through his mind again: house plus high school equals Cynthia. Well, better late than never. And better early than late.

"Are you busy?" asked Cynthia, smiling.

"Not that busy," Ellery assured her. "Won't you come in? I'm just finishing up my caviar."

She came in, and Ellery closed the door. She was wearing a dark green skirt and a white silk blouse, and her blond hair was down. She was slim and tanned and she looked good.

Very good.

"Now that you're a reporter," she said, "I thought I'd bring you a story."

"Fine," said Ellery. "Bring it on into the kitchen and I'll give you a beer for a reward."

She followed him into the kitchen and sat down at the table, wrinkling her nose slightly at the hamburger. She accepted the beer without complaint, but she didn't look like the beer-drinking type.

"Sorry I don't have anything better," Ellery said. "I just moved in here, and I haven't stocked the cellar yet. In fact, I haven't got a cellar."

She laughed gently. It was a pleasant laugh. It said: "That wasn't a bit funny, but it was a reasonable try."

"Do you eat hamburgers every night?" Cynthia asked.

"Not at all," Ellery assured her. "I fry a mean egg too, so there's no monotony in my diet."

"Poor man," Cynthia said. "You need a cook. Will I do?"

There it was. No stalling, no fumbling for invitations, no beating around the bush. Cynthia wasn't being coy, and she wasn't kidding. Ellery decided that he and Cynthia were going to get along fine.

"Lady," he said, "you will do splendidly. I won't even ask for references."

"That's good," she said, "because I haven't got any."

Ellery finished his beer and opened another. "When do we start this charming arrangement?" he asked.

Cynthia smiled her man-killer smile. "Let's make it tomorrow night," she suggested. "I'll bring the groceries and see if I can impress you."

"With or without groceries," Ellery assured her, "you will impress me."

"Good," said Cynthia. She crossed her legs pleasantly. "Let's not forget about the story, Paul."

Ellery, who had done just that, nodded. He went into the living room and got an empty notebook. "Let's have it," he said, sitting down again. "I'll phone Stubbs and have him stop the presses."

"No hurry," Cynthia said. "It's about the high school. It opens on the third of September, and all new students will have to have a birth certificate, small-pox vaccination, and diphtheria immunization."

Ellery stared at her. She wasn't fooling, so he wrote it down. He remembered that Cynthia taught home economics in the high school. My God, maybe she *was* going to cook him a dinner!

Period.

"That all?" he asked.

"That's all." She smiled. "I just thought I'd save you a little work."

"Well, thanks. Thanks a lot."

Ellery took a long pull on his beer. Just when you thought you had these people all figured out they always pulled another rabbit out of the hat.

No matter. Cynthia could be useful. Anyway, he liked rabbits.

"Cynthia," he said, "I wonder if you'd tell me something."

"I'm sure you do," Cynthia said.

Ellery ignored that one. "Look," he said earnestly, "I'm in a tough spot here—you know that. You're about the only person I've met who's acted—well, who's acted—"

"Human?" Cynthia suggested.

"Friendly," Ellery corrected. "I don't feel so much like a freak when you're around."

Cynthia laughed. "What do you want to know, Paul?"

Ellery put it on the line: he had a nagging suspicion that it would be a stupid man indeed who thought he could put over a fast one on Cynthia. "I saw a notice in the paper, last week's paper," he said, "about a compulsory something at the Thorne Ranch the day after tomorrow. I saw you out there, and I wonder——"

"What it's all about," finished Cynthia. She patted her hair.

"Check," said Ellery. "If I'm going to play on your team, I've got to know the signals."

Cynthia pursed her lips. "I don't know, Paul," she said. "I'd like to tell you, but I'm not sure that it's permitted. Tell you what I'll do, though—I'll find out just where you stand on this, and if I can get an okay I'll do better than explain it. I'll take you out there with me, and you can watch."

"Fair enough, Cynthia. Thanks."

She finished her beer and stood up. "We'll see what we see," she said. "Thanks for the beer. Have to run now."

"So soon?"

"So soon." She walked toward the door, the green skirt rustling around her legs.

Ellery caught her at the door, touched her cool arm with his hand. He could smell the perfume in her hair.

"Cynthia——"

"Good night, Paul," she said, softly but firmly. "See you tomorrow."

And she was gone, into the gathering shadows of night.

10

NEXT MORNING, Paul Ellery was up early. It was still cool from the night before, but the sun was already climbing into the sky for the day's bombardment.

However, he did notice, on his way to the newspaper office, that there were just the bare suggestions of gray clouds hanging on the horizon. They might mean nothing, but there was a chance they spelled a break in the heat. August was a hot month in Texas, but usually the rains came in by September. They were long overdue.

The cadaverous Mr. Stubbs had not yet arrived, so Ellery went into his office and hacked out a story on the high school's opening He finished just as Stubbs came in, and he took it in and placed it on his desk.

A. Jeremiah Stubbs looked at him as he might have looked at a stray goldfish in his drinking water and said nothing. Very carefully, he took off his shapeless black coat and hung it on the hook on his door. He then rolled up his sleeves, freeing his white, skinny arms for action, and donned his green eye shade. His work for the day presumably finished, he lowered himself wearily into his swivel chair behind the editor's desk and resumed his fascinated contemplation of the empty wall.

"If you don't have anything urgent that needs doing," Ellery said, "I'm going out to look for some news."

Mr. Stubbs gazed at him in mild astonishment. He blinked his eyes as though he had difficulty keeping him in focus. "Look for news?" he repeated.

Ellery nodded.

Mr. Stubbs concentrated mightily and one corner of his upper lip twitched. The unaccustomed smile almost fractured his jaw. "Only one real story in this town, sonny," he said, "and that's the one we can't print."

Ellery waited respectfully, but that was all there was. Mr. Stubbs spoke mainly in silences, and it was up to his listener to figure out the drift of his inaudible conversations. Having no real evidence either way, Ellery again chose to interpret the silence as approval, and so he left. In truth, there was very little that needed to be done on *The Jefferson Springs Watchguard*, and Paul Ellery found it hard to take the job too seriously.

There must be something more than this.

And yet, weren't there still the tiresome little jobs filled by colorless people, even in interstellar civilizations? Surely not *everybody* spent his time cruising around in spaceships. If Earth joined the galactic league, wouldn't someone still have to work in the gas station, clerk in the grocery store, take tickets at the movie?

Ellery drove home, without the vaguest intention of looking for any news. He had his own work to do. He noticed hopefully that the gray clouds were massed more thickly on the horizon. It might—just *might*—rain.

At home, he sat down at the kitchen table and sipped his

coffee. Everything was happening so fast that it was getting away from him. He didn't like the prospect of getting swept along by the current. He wanted to steer a little.

What did he, as an anthropologist, know that might help him in the life he found himself living?

The cards were all stacked against him in Jefferson Springs, no matter how much the dealer smiled. If he wanted a wild card in his hand, he would have to pull it out of his own sleeve. If he wanted to win, or only to break even——

The first step was finding the right question to ask. After that, he had to be able to recognize the answer when he saw it.

Well, this was clearly a problem in culture contact, and that had a name: acculturation. Unhappily, however, the problem wasn't really an acculturation problem. Of the two cultures—correction, more than two; this thing wasn't limited to the United States—one was unaware of the contact!

And, in a very real sense, they weren't in contact.

Still, *he* was in an acculturation situation. He was a savage, rubbing his nose in civilization. The principles of acculturation must apply to him as well as to all the other primitive peoples who had found themselves in the same boat. Could he make the jump, blowgun to atom bomb? Cave to skyscraper?

What were the choices open to him?

He sweated it out. There had been a great deal of work done on problems of acculturation, but very little of it seemed applicable to the fix he was in. Facts were more insistent than theories: his thoughts constantly returned to Two Bears, his old interpreter. He had done his first field work among the Hawk Indians of Montana, and he had made many friends there. The Hawks were a former Plains tribe, with the customary bison-hunting economy, and they had never taken too kindly to agriculture. The old people still had a security of a sort, living in the past. But the younger men and women were trapped between the old and the new. Two Bears was inclined to be a little contemptuous of the ways of his ancestors, and in any event their culture was practically extinct. At the same time, he was enough of an Indian, culturally speaking, so that he didn't fit into the pattern of American life around him.

Two Bears was a very mixed-up man, trying to fit fragments of opposing lifeways together into a meaningful whole.

He spent a lot of time getting drunk. He spent a lot of time, too, off in the hills by himself—alone with the gods that he could not quite accept.

Paul Ellery understood him a little better now.

He took a fast, cold shower, and shaved too quickly, nicking himself twice. He got dressed, abandoning his work clothes for a pair of brown slacks, white shirt, and tie, and loafers with noisy yellow argyle socks.

At a quarter after six, Cynthia drove up outside.

He lifted two large sacks out of the front seat and carried them into the house, setting them down on the kitchen table. One clinked and one didn't.

"I didn't expect you to have an apron," Cynthia said, "so I brought one of my own." She took a plastic apron out of her purse and tied it around her hips. "Now you get out of here, and I'll start supper."

"Yes, master," Paul Ellery said. He walked into the living room and sat down, reflecting that of all the mysteries in Jefferson Springs Cynthia certainly wasn't the least. He fired up his pipe and listened to Cynthia's heels clicking around in the kitchen. He timed her. In fifteen minutes flat she was out, a glass in each hand.

"I hope you like Martinis," she said, handing him one.

"I'm enchanted," Ellery said. He examined his glass. "And two olives! You've read my mind."

"No," Cynthia said seriously. "Just guessed."

She sat down next to him on the couch. Ellery could feel his pulse thudding like a schoolboy's, but he let it thud. He couldn't figure Cynthia out, and for now he was content to let it go at that. Of course, it was flattering to think that he was just plain irresistible, but if that were the case then he could think of a large number of females in the past who must have been blind.

Cynthia had on a smooth but simple black dress, nothing fancy, and she had a green ribbon in her soft blond hair. Her dress caught the light and rustled when she moved, and she seemed quite conscious of the effect.

Ellery sipped his Martini, which was extremely dry and extremely potent. "What did you find out about tomorrow night?" he asked. "Am I included out?"

Cynthia patted his knee. "Not at all, Paul," she said. "I talked to John and he fixed it up. You can come."

"You know John?"

"Of course. Have another?"

"Sold."

She went back into the kitchen, bustled around a bit, and came back with two fresh Martinis. This time, his had three olives in it.

"This," Paul Ellery said sincerely, "is the life. I'm converted. Where do I go to enlist?"

"I'm not trying to sell you anything, Paul," Cynthia said,

with a directness he found disconcerting. "I'm here on my own. Wait until tomorrow night, then see what you think of us."

"What *happens* out there tomorrow? Black Mass?"

She laughed, the Martini putting a flush in her cheeks. "Not exactly," she said. She had nice white teeth. "It's sort of a—well, sort of a ceremony. Only not exactly that. Not a ritual either, really. And not quite a political meeting. It—draws us together, all of us, on all the worlds. Do you understand that, Paul?"

"Not exactly," Ellery admitted. "But I'll say Rite of Intensification; that sounds good."

"To tell the truth," Cynthia said, downing her Martini, "I think the whole thing is kind of corny."

There it was again. The offbeat note. The wrong chord. If these people would just be human or alien, one or the other, it wouldn't be so bad. But when they were both—

"You won't find it corny, though," Cynthia added. "I promise you that. The first time is apt to be—uncomfortable."

"You hold my hand," Ellery suggested. "I won't be scared."

"We'll see," Cynthia said. "And now we'll eat."

She vanished into the kitchen again. Five minutes later she called him, and there it was. Thick steaks covered with mushrooms. Mashed potatoes with natural gravy. A crisp green salad. A glass of cold water and another Martini.

Ellery pitched in. "By God," he said, "you *can* cook."

"I have my talents," Cynthia said, and met his eyes without wavering.

After supper, with the dishes stacked in the sink and another Martini under his belt, Ellery was feeling amorous.

"And now," Cynthia said, "we cool off a little. Let's take a walk."

"Walk?"

"Walk."

They walked.

They walked under a darkening sky, through a hushed and breathless night. They walked along the street toward town, arm in arm, like any two lovers since time began.

He thought: *just like two average people in an average sort of town. How could you doubt it?*

Cynthia was warm and soft in his arm. They walked down past the icehouse and across the tracks. Ellery could smell the orange trees, their fragrance suspended in the electric air. They turned to the right and walked on into Mexican Town. The pavement ended, and they walked on a dirt road, like a path, but there were more lights now, and laughter floated out of the night.

Someone, somewhere, was strumming a guitar. The sound was happy, and a little lonely too.

They passed several Mexican couples, strolling along, talking in Spanish. The Mexicans nodded, friendly but reserved. They were better dressed than the native Texans of the town; the men with ties and sport clothes, the women with bright, flowing dresses that were designed to please. Ellery liked them, as he had always liked Mexico.

A distant rumble ruffled the still air. The night tensed itself, waiting.

"These people," Ellery said quietly. "Are they—part of it?"

Cynthia laughed, her voice faintly husky. "Yes, Paul. They're part of it too, all of them."

"But—well, are they happy here? I mean, the lot of most

Mexicans in Texas leaves something to be desired. I'd think that people of your civilization——"

She squeezed his arm. "You can't understand us yet, can you? Paul, there are all sorts of physical types in the universe. On one planet, one type is running the show, and somewhere else it's a different group. It's purely a matter of historical accident, and if you *know* that, it doesn't matter. These people know that they're just as good as we are, and we know it too, so the tension isn't there. It isn't where you live that counts, it's how other people think of you. We go where we can, and live as we must."

"Thanks for the anthropology lesson."

"You're welcome, love."

There was a deeper hush, sudden and complete. Then the thunder crashed, and there was no doubt about it this time. A small, cool breeze began to whimper along the street.

"We'd better get back," Ellery said.

"Yes. Come on."

They walked back down the dirt road, and back to the paved highway again. They crossed the tracks and hurried past the big square icehouse, squatting like a cement monster in the darkness. They could see the lightning now, flashing down in livid forks out of the massed black clouds that blotted out the stars. The thunder was a continuous rumble in the north.

They walked faster, and the wet breeze became a wind, sighing down the street. The smell of rain clogged the air, rich and sweet and heavy.

Ellery rolled up the windows in Cynthia's Nash, and they half ran up to the little porch of his house.

They just made it.

There was a flash of lightning that charged the air, quick and close and turning the night into pale silver. Then the thunder that crashed down, splitting the skies. A gathering, a hush, a pause——

And then the rain.

Sheets of it, smashing down in big fat drops. Buckets and tubs and rivers of it, gushing into the dry gray street. The street glistened and little brooks gurgled down the gutters.

Ellery caught his breath, his arm holding Cynthia close. The lightning flashed and flickered and the thunder rolled The storm roared in from the desert wastes, and the wind and the rain washed through the streets of Jefferson Springs.

They went inside and closed the door behind them. The storm pattered and surged on the roof, and the air was released and fresh. Ellery flicked on the light.

Cynthia smiled at him and Ellery could feel the tightness in his stomach, the blood in his veins.

She reached up, slowly, and untied the green ribbon in her hair. She shook her hair gently and it caressed her shoulders. He could smell its subtle perfume.

She came to him and loosened his necktie, her hands cool and sure.

"Well," she whispered softly, "what are you waiting for, Paul?"

11

NEXT MORNING, it was still raining—a gentle rain now, that pattered against the window panes and splashed into little puddles off the roof. Thunder muttered furtively, far away and lonely, rumbling around on the horizon, looking for a way back to town.

Cynthia was already up and dressed when Ellery opened his eyes, and he could smell breakfast cooking in the kitchen. He lay quietly for a long minute, sniffing the rich aroma of percolating coffee and the fresh tang of frying bacon, and then he eased himself out of bed and into his bathrobe.

He felt good. He felt better than he had felt in a long time. He told himself that he was certainly satisfied, and probably happy.

Still, he wasn't positive he liked everything he remembered about the night just past.

What do you want, boy, he thought, *egg in your beer?*

When he walked into the kitchen, after more or less combing his hair, Cynthia had her back to him, frying eggs. Her blond hair was tied back again with the green ribbon and she looked cool, beautiful, and collected. He kissed her on the ear and she smiled.

"I think I'll call you Cyn for short," Ellery said. "Spelled with an 's' and an 'i' and an 'n.'"

"I'm flattered, Paul. Two eggs or three?"

"Make it three," Ellery said. He found himself feeling playful, but he sensed that Cynthia wasn't having any.

Breakfast it was, then.

"Will the rain hurt things tonight?" he asked, working on his second cup of coffee.

"Not too much, Paul, unless it rains harder than it's raining this morning. It's too important to call off, you know. They'll be electing delegates."

"Delegates?"

"You'll see. You mustn't be impatient, love."

"Okay. All things come to him who waits, so I'm told."

"Well," said Cynthia, "you wait for me this evening and we'll test your proverb."

"You can't stay?"

"Sorry. You know I'd like to. But I've got—things—to do before tonight. Can you wash the dishes and make the bed? I'll be back for you about eight."

"Fair enough," said Ellery.

Cynthia got to her feet and smoothed her dress down over her hips. She picked up her purse and glanced at her watch.

"Cyn?"

"Yes?"

"Is anything wrong? You seem so—well, different."

Cynthia put her purse down. She came to him and put her arms around his neck. She kissed him, hard and expertly.

Her body was cool as silk, and Ellery began to tremble. She let him go and smiled, her white teeth very sharp.

"See you at eight, love. Don't forget about me."

Ellery laughed, a little hoarsely, and she was gone. Ellery stood at the door and watched her drive away. The blue Nash turned left at the high school and vanished into the gray mist.

The gray day darkened and became night, and still the drizzle came. There was more rain in the sky, more real rain, but it was holding off.

Waiting.

Ellery found himself afraid again, and stuck the .38 in his pants pocket. He hoped it wouldn't show under the raincoat.

Exactly at eight o'clock, Cynthia came back. He had hoped that she would come in, but she honked the horn for him and he went out. The street was glistening under the car's headlights.

"All set?" she asked.

"All set," he said. He wished that it were true.

The Nash purred off through the drizzle, its windshield wipers ticking and shushing against the tiny, hesitant rain-spray. Cynthia looked inviting as ever, in brown slacks and a gray sweater, with a raincoat tossed over her shoulders; but she seemed distant and preoccupied, so Ellery didn't try to talk.

It was hard to believe that just sixteen hours ago——

Well, the hell with it. Ellery watched the yellow head-lights cut wetly through the town, licking at the empty glass windows and the pale gasoline pumps, and then they were on the highway, the tires hissing through the dampness.

Before he was really ready, they were at the Thorne Ranch. They got out. There were already at least one hundred cars parked around the ranch yard, glistening dully in the drizzle, but otherwise the ranch looked normal enough. There weren't even any lights on inside. The cars in the yard might have been sitting in a parking lot outside a fair or a stock show or a football game.

Cynthia set off with a quick, determined stride, out across a wet field, away from the ranch buildings. Ellery, feeling rather like a faithful dog curious about a missing bone, turned up his coat collar and followed her dark shadow. The soaking rain of the previous night hadn't been a drop in the bucket to the thirsty fields, and the ground was not muddy, although it was a trifle slick.

The thunder rumbled distantly, promising to do better.

They worked their way along toward a bend in the river, and Ellery could sense other figures moving along with them through the night. They topped a slight rise, too small to qualify as a hill, and at first there was nothing.

And then there it was.

It was a large square of pale blue lights, invisible until you were almost on top of them. Pale blue lights, like glowing, bloated bugs hanging in the mist. Beyond them, the poplars and cypress that fringed the river made a black wall. Inside them was the population of Jefferson Springs, Texas.

They were all there, or soon would be. All six thousand of them. Ellery's first reaction was one of surprise—surprise that a whole town could fit in that pale blue square. But then he recalled that it was nothing for fifty or sixty thousand to watch a football game.

There seemed to be a screen of some sort around the square, a wall of invisible force. Cynthia had to take his hand and lead him through. The citizens of Jefferson Springs stood quietly, waiting. A few had brought along canvas chairs. The people were all different in their attitudes. Ellery saw old women, dressed in black funeral dresses, who were rapt and consecrated. He saw wide-eyed children, and children who clearly had their minds on other things. He saw thoughtful men, impatient men, bored men. One portly gentleman with a cigar was loudly issuing orders that nobody listened to.

And there was Mr. Stubbs, looking gloomy. Clearly, Stubbs expected a hurricane at any moment. He was prepared to be blown away.

Ellery started to relax a little. Nothing alarming here. Just like a big meeting, or even a picnic.

The music started.

It was soft, subtle, insidious. Ellery couldn't see where it was coming from. It throbbed and beat softly, almost inaudibly. You had to strain to hear it, and yet you couldn't get away from it. It was inside your head—searching.

Ellery thought of stars.

He heard the voices now. People were talking. They weren't talking English; they were speaking their own language. It had tones and buzzes and clicks.

Ellery shivered. He wished that it hadn't been quite so dark. The pale blue lights tricked the eyes. He wished that it would start to rain. Really rain. He would like to hear rain now.

"I'll have to leave you," Cynthia's voice said. Hers was the only voice speaking in English. "Enjoy yourself, love."

She was gone. He was alone. He had never been so alone. The music began to beat at him. The pale blue lights began to blur. Sweat trickled down under his arms, icily. He was afraid to move.

A hand touched him on the elbow.

Ellery crouched without thinking, his hand clutching for

the butt of his .38. He almost drew it out, and then he saw who it was.

A jovial little fat man with shrewd, laughing eyes.

John.

"Still hunting monsters, Paul?" he whispered.

"No. Sorry! Yes. Dammit, am I glad to see *you!*"

"Not so loud, old man. You just try to keep your eyes open, and I'll cue you in when I can on what is going on. Deal?"

"Deal," agreed Ellery gratefully.

A pickup truck came jouncing across the field toward the square of blue lights, feeling its way with only its parking lights on. It came inside and two men unloaded a large metallic box. They placed it carefully on the ground in the middle of the square. It had no connections, dials, knobs, or levers of any kind, as far as Ellery could make out. It was just a box.

All the lights winked out but one blue eye, staring at him. The beat of the music throbbed through his veins.

"News report," John whispered.

The box talked.

It talked for perhaps fifteen minutes. The voice was not unduly loud, but it had a compelling quality to it. Ellery could not understand a word of it, but it did not *sound* terribly different from an ordinary news summary coming over an ordinary radio.

John whispered: "More attention promised for colonials . . . that old bunk . . . some economic difficulties in Capella Sector . . . a scrunch play won the Sequences; you wouldn't get that . . . a new treaty with the Transformists . . . a suspected sighting of the Others . . . a Two Representative says there is corruption in Arcturus Sector . . . some guff

about the traditional planetwide conference coming up in Sol
Sector; that's a special tossed on the line to inflate our egos—
they'll never hear it outside the system . . . the Evolutionaries agree to a compromise on Spicus Six, just opened up
. . . the usual stuff."

Oh sure. The usual stuff.

The box stopped.

A smooth-shaven, portly man moved to the center of the
square. Ellery recognized him as Samuel Cartwright, mayor
of Jefferson Springs. He began to talk persuasively in the
alien tongue—persuasively, but with just a hint of a lisp that
Ellery had noticed before, as though Cartwright were having
trouble with his false teeth. He talked for ten minutes, paus-
ing now and then to wipe the mist from his face.

When he stopped, there was scattered finger-snapping,
which Ellery took to be applause, and several quite Earthly
catcalls. A lively wrangle ensued, and some of the citizens
appeared to be getting hot under the collar.

Clearly, they were electing some representatives.

"Delegates to the big conference," John whispered, con-
firming Ellery's guess. "They're going to discuss our colonial
policy toward Earth. Want to come?"

"You're kidding," Ellery said.

"Not at all, Paul. I can fix it up. I carry some weight
around here, you know. Anyway, it's high time you got an
education. I'll notify you."

The election was over, with two men and a woman picked
to represent Jefferson Springs. Ellery waited, wondering what
was coming next. For a long minute, there was nothing.

The people, however, were very quiet. Ellery could hear
the tiny ticks of the rain on his coat. Suddenly, the one blue
light winked out. There was total darkness. The beat of the

music, almost forgotten, picked up. It grew stronger, much stronger.

And stronger still.

Ellery felt himself swaying on his feet and tried to steady himself.

"Don't fight it, Paul," came John's voice from far away.

He was floating on a gray cloud, a warm gray cloud. He could feel the cloud in his hands. He could pick it up and shred it like cotton.

He drifted, lost and entranced.

He saw colors, smelled smells, tasted tastes. He spun lazily, a moth in the summer night, swallowed in euphoria.

He saw his home with a strange, distorted clarity. He smelled fried chicken in the kitchen. He saw his old books on the shelf in the room he had grown up in: *The Wind in the Willows, Just-So Stories, The Wizard of Oz.* He saw his old model airplanes suspended from the ceiling, their tissue-paper wings shredding where the glue was wearing off. He saw his mother, young again, and his father, snorting at the evening paper.

The scene shifted, noiselessly and completely. He was playing football for the Austin Maroons, racing down the green field under the lights. He heard the crowd, on its feet and yelling. He shook off one tackler, throwing a hip into him, and angled off to his right. The broken strap on his rib pads twisted sweatily. He saw that he wasn't going to make it past the safety man, who wasn't going to be faked out of the way. He set himself to run over him, fighting for the extra yard, and then there was a *smack* as the safety man went down in a heap, blocked out by his end. He cut for the goal stripe. He was going all the way——

Again the scene shifted. He caught his breath. There

was a planet, a blue and green and brown planet, hanging like a jewel in black velvet. It was his planet. His vision flickered, and the scene expanded fantastically. His field of sight was enormous, vast beyond imagination, and yet the whole thing was crystal-clear. There were many suns, and many planets. Together, they formed a Titanic design that he could barely grasp. Between the worlds, almost invisible, were spun gossamer silver threads, tying them together. Atoms, atoms of worlds——

Something else. Something down in the corner, down dark in the corner. Something vague, amorphous—

He wanted to scream. Perhaps he did. He whirled, twisted, spun. Dizziness and mist. . . .

It was over. He blinked his eyes and saw that John was holding him up. The blue light snapped back on. The spray of rain cooled his forehead.

"All right?"

"I—think so."

"It's a little strange at first. You didn't get it all, old man. Designed to reinforce, do you see, rather than to dramatize. You've got to supply most of the images, and you won't see what the others see until you go to a Center and get the full treatment. You should have picked up the drift, though: nostalgia for home, the relation of the one to the many, the unity of civilized life— that sort of thing. Quite unimaginative, really."

Ellery listened to John's clipped, matter-of-fact voice and was more than ever grateful to him for being on hand. The rotund little man with the fringe of hair around his pink skull looked like a worldly friar out of Chaucer. He was something solid and real to hang onto. He was a man you could deal with as a man, without worrying about culture or status or formalities. In a word, Ellery thought, John was one hell of a good guy.

An old woman, gray-haired and earnest, stood up in the glow of the blue lights and intoned some syllables, letting them collapse from her thin lips in monotonous cadences. There was considerable shuffling of feet among the audience.

"Poem," said John. "Very bad."

The old woman sat down. The blue lights brightened, almost imperceptibly. The music switched its key. It sounded proud, and a little sad. It swelled up in stirring sweeps, suggesting ancient kings and magnificent temples and acts of bravery long forgotten.

"You'll get more of this," John whispered. "It's the first landing here, the first colonists."

The music pounded, then faded to a low murmur.

The blue lights dimmed, and then began to brighten again, very slowly and steadily.

The people chanted, their voices filling the great night silences.

Ellery saw Earth through alien eyes—wonderful, mysterious, frightening, compelling.

He saw a hidden ship in the night, a globe that floated down in a deserted field, a handful of colonists turned loose near a waiting car. The men and women alone in a strange world, ready to carve a life for themselves out of a primitive planet.

The colonists walked to the car, got inside. They were well trained and they knew what to do, how to move in. They were part of a superlatively well-organized immigration. They knew every step they had to make.

Still, they were afraid.

This was a new world for them, a new home, a chance for their children. They were pioneers in an occupied land.

The car started. They drove toward town, a square of lights far away but clear in the clean, cool air. They were dressed like the natives, they looked like the natives, they talked like the natives. They were ready, and their eyes shone with a hard determination.

They must not fail.

They *would* not fail.

The car purred on down the highway, through a strange and marvellous land. . . .

The music stopped. The chant died. Ellery opened his eyes.

He saw them all around him, the people of Jefferson Springs, ghostly in the pale blue light and the drizzle of the rain. The people of Jefferson Springs, the colonists—proud, confident, superior.

And, somehow, a million million miles away.

Ellery felt sick and tired. He was not a part of them. He was not *one* of them. He was just——

Nothing.

Nobody.

He looked at Cynthia, on the other side of the square. Blond hair, blue eyes, brown slacks, gray sweater, a raincoat tossed over her shoulders. She was lost in pride. She was smiling, as a queen might smile. She was *somebody*. She didn't even look at him. She wouldn't have seen him if she had.

He felt John's firm hand on his arm. There were words. He felt the field, moist and earthy under his feet. A car, and the highway again. His house, dark and empty and alone.

"You'll be all right, Paul."

"I know."

"It takes a little time."

"Sure."

"I'll be back in a few days."

"Thanks, John."

John was gone. He went inside and turned on the lights. He threw himself down on the couch in the living room. He lay very still and listened to the cold sound of thunder rumbling in from the other side of the world.

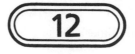

12

SLEEP DID NOT COME.

At three in the morning he got up, changed his clothes, packed a bag and left. It was cool in the morning mist, and very dark. He started his car and drove out of Jefferson Springs. By five, he was through San Antonio, circling by way of Loop 13. He stopped to get gas, drank a coke, and drove on down the Austin highway.

He was not quitting. He knew he would go back. But right now he needed a break.

He needed Anne.

He smiled a little. He always ran to Anne when he was in trouble, and Anne was always there. Someday, she wouldn't be. He knew that. No girl would wait forever.

But that was in the other world.

By half-past six, he was in Austin. It was sultry already, and he opened all the windows. He drove past Hill's—how many steaks had he eaten at Hill's?—and past Irving's, and crossed the bridge over the Colorado River. He drove down the broad sweep of Congress Avenue, almost deserted in the early-morning gloom. He stopped at the P-K Grill, which was open all night, and drank three cups of coffee. Then he drove down and parked on the corner, across from the Capitol Dome, and just sat. Anne wouldn't be up yet, and he didn't want to go home.

He watched the city wake up. Austin was his city. He tried to remember that. It wasn't easy.

The sky lightened to a gray glare. He looked back down Congress. Humphrey Bogart at the State, James Stewart at the Paramount, Roy Rogers at the Queen. The bulk of the Austin Hotel dominating the street. Shoe stores, department stores, ten-cent stores, banks, cafes, offices. The Capitol Building, with its big Lone Star Flag. Newspapers stacked on the corners. And—yes, there was Norman, the thinnest and most energetic newspaper seller in the United States, already hawking the morning headlines. How many papers had he bought from Norman, over on the Drag in front of the University?

The cars came first, and then the people. The cars dribbled down the street in the beginning, fed into Congress Avenue by a network of side streets. As the sun climbed higher into the leaden sky, the cars came faster. They squirted into the street, and then flowed like rivers, compressed and controlled by the dams of traffic lights. The horns honked, the brakes screeched, the gears ground. Hot-rods and motor-cycles charged up and down the street with a clatter and a bang, and vacant-eyed female drivers consistently managed to turn right from the left lanes. By eight o'clock, the first ambulance had moaned through the street, scattering the cars like toys. Somewhere, energetically, a cop blew a whistle.

The people seeped out of the walls. At first, there had been only a scattered few: a neatly dressed man with a cane, who was undoubtedly never late to his office; a pale woman gazing into store windows; a tired young man in need of a shave who had come hurriedly out of a hotel via the side entrance. Then, as though the few had divided like cells to become many, the sidewalks were jammed. Big ones, little ones, fat ones, thin ones. A blind man sitting hopefully with his box of pencils. A girl and her mother getting new clothes for school. The lights clicked through their memorized routine, and human beings and cars took turns testing the pavement.

The heat hit like a bombardment. It was an unseasonal, humid heat. The hot air was caught between the cement and the gray clouds. Whatever god was responsible for such matters fumbled around for the rain trigger and couldn't find it.

Ellery felt choked, and his hands were shaking. His hair felt sticky. His eyes burned. He felt like hell.

It wasn't all the heat.

He looked at his city and didn't recognize it. The city had changed. It had been comfortable and soft and familiar. It was now distressing, hard, and alien.

It was a reservation for savages.

It *had* changed—if only in his mind. And he had changed, too. He wasn't the same Paul Ellery who had left Austin to spend the summer justifying a research grant. He didn't quite know what to make of Paul Ellery Number Two. He did know one thing: he wasn't very comfortable to live with.

He started the car and drove slowly out past the University of Texas, a collection of vaguely Spanish structures dominated and presided over by a white skyscraper with a Greek temple perched in perpetual surprise on top of it, and on to the greenish apartment house on King Street where Anne lived.

He went up the outside stairs and rang the bell. There was a short pause and the door opened. It wasn't Anne.

"Paulsy!" exclaimed Peg, Anne's eternal roommate. "My dear, you look like the *wrahth of Gawd*, I mean you *really* do."

"Thank you, Dale Carnegie," Ellery said. "Is Anne around?"

"But of *coawse!* Come in for heaven's sakes, I'll *call* her."

"Fine," said Ellery. He walked inside and slumped in the chair by the phonograph.

"Now you be careful of my etchings," Peg said. "They smear *dreadfully.*"

"No more rug-weaving?"

"Oh, heavens no! I gave that up months ago. Paulsy, it's so good to see you."

"It's good to see you too, Peg," Ellery said, and he meant it.

Peg disappeared to attempt the Herculean feat of waking Anne up, and Ellery reflected that he had always liked Peg, and didn't quite know why. She was a dizzy blonde, not devastating but well informed, and she had an arty personality that in anyone else he would have detested cordially. But Peg never took herself any more seriously than she deserved, and she was one of those curious and wonderful people who were always just "around" when you particularly needed a friend. You had to take Peg on her own terms, but she wore well.

Ellery took in the well-remembered apartment with real affection, and felt himself beginning to relax a little. There were books all over the place, and they were stacked in untidy piles that indicated they were being read instead of exhibited.

But the place was clean, comfortable, and quiet. It was

subtly feminine, with unexpected frills and flowers popping out here and there, but its sex wasn't flaunted. It was an apartment resigned to being a girl, and enjoying it, but still given to playing tomboy now and then.

There was a swish and Anne was in his arms.

"Ell," she whispered. "I've been so lonesome."

"Me too," said Ellery.

He looked at her, holding her at arm's length. Her dark hair was mussed and she didn't have any make-up on. Only her clear gray-green eyes hinted that she could be beautiful when she wanted to. She had on a shapeless blue bathrobe, and from underneath it peeked a sleazy pink silk nightgown. Anne's pet vice was an addiction to secret-agent nightgowns and harem pajamas, and Ellery had never objected yet.

"You look good," he said. "You look wonderful."

"You don't, Ell. I love you, but you look shot. Want some breakfast?"

"I could use some."

Anne went into the kitchen, taking Ellery with her. She brewed up sausages and poached eggs and toast and coffee. Suspecting a hangover, she made a quart of orange juice and made him drink most of it. He did feel better when he finished, and his nervousness turned into weariness.

"Now, you lazy man," she said, kissing him lightly, "You're going to bed. I've got to work this afternoon, and tonight we're going out. I refuse to go out with somnambulists. I'll wake you up when I get home."

She put him to bed, firmly. She kissed him again, picked up clothes from various places, and disappeared into the bathroom to get dressed. Ellery stretched, feeling tired and delighted.

He heard Anne come out of the bathroom after a while,

and he heard her phone somebody named Ralph and break her date for that night. He heard the door open and she sneaked in and kissed his nose.

"Good night, or good day or something," she whispered. "Nice to have you back in the house of ill-repute."

"Night, hon," he said. "I think I love you."

"What, again? It must have been something you ate."

And she was gone. Peg had kept discreetly out of the way, and he didn't know whether or not she was still in the apartment. He yawned, hugely.

Jefferson Springs seemed far, far away.

He slept.

Hours later, he awoke when Anne shook his shoulder. "Rise and shine, handsome," she said. "You're taking me out to supper tonight, or didn't you know?"

"I didn't know," Ellery mumbled. "I thought perhaps your magic touch in the kitchen——"

"No thanks, pal. I get tired, you know—it's one of my little idiosyncracies. If I'm supposed to be charming, gay, and lovable tonight, then you're supposed to dig down in the vault and buy me some eats."

"I'll pay," Ellery said. "Don't beat me any more."

They changed clothes and went out to Irving's, where they disposed of two charcoal-broiled filets. Then they drove out to Lake Austin and stopped at the Flamingo. It was still hot and overcast, with no stars in sight. They bought a fifth of Scotch from the adjoining liquor store before going inside—the quaint Texas liquor laws ruling mixed drinks evil and corrupting unless you bring your own fifth and pour it in yourself.

They got a quiet booth at the Flamingo, held hands, and Ellery settled down to some serious drinking. The Flamingo was pleasant and modern, and its most distinctive attribute was a painting of a sensational nude, which hung over the piano. Confirmed barflies had a legend that after twenty-five beers, no more and no less, you could watch closely and see the nude roll over. Ellery had tried it one time, in his younger days, but had been rewarded with only a slight twitch of the right shoulder.

It seemed that everyone in the Flamingo knew Anne, and stopped to say hello. Anne was a girl with a lovely split personality. About half the time she was the gayest of the party-party crowd, and the other half she holed up in her apartment and read. Ellery was about the only man who had seen both sides of her character, which gave him a certain distinction.

"Anything wrong, Ell?"

"Wrong? Of course not."

"You're the worst liar I know. I must remember that. What is it—work going badly, bored with me again, just ornery?"

"Ornery, I guess. Let's pretend it isn't there, okay?"

"Okay. Laugh and be merry, for tomorrow we will have hangovers."

She was merry, too, at least on the outside. She took Ellery in hand, made him dance, and poured Scotch into him. It was a therapy that had worked before, and tonight it was *almost* successful. Except that Ellery got too high.

He took to monopolizing the jukebox, feeding it with handfuls of quarters. He started out with good swing, showing marked favoritism to records cut prior to the bop mania, and then, with more Scotch, proceeded to sloppy ballads that would have sickened him if he had been sober.

"I love you, Annie," he said along about midnight. "I really love you. You're the finest, sweetest——"

"There, there," Anne said, patting his hand. "You always love me when you're drunk. You love everybody when you're drunk."

Ellery downed another drink, hurrying to get it in before the midnight curfew. "I don't know about that," he said slowly. "I just don't *know* about that." He was feeling very wise and lucid. "It's my theory that drink reveals a man's character. You see, Annie, when I get drunk I *do* love everybody. I love *everybody*. You see?"

"That's wonderful," Anne said.

"You *do* see. You see, if *everybody* loved everybody when everybody was drunk, you see, why then, everybody . . . everybody . . ."

"I see," Anne said, as Ellery trailed off into uncharted vistas of the mind.

Finally, Ellery surged to his feet. "We go!" he announced.

"Goody," said Anne. She carefully picked up her purse and tipped the waitress.

Ellery set himself in motion toward the door. He was confident that he had never walked with more dignity. Anne artfully removed a forgotten paper napkin from his belt to add to the illusion. He paused once before the jukebox and listened with great concentration.

"Terrific," he announced, after due deliberation. And then, at the top of his lungs, he added: "Oh, play that THING!"

Anne steered him to the car and shortly they were home.

Ellery mounted the stairs, singing lustily, and carried Anne over the threshold into her own apartment. He dropped her on the floor, missing the chair with great precision, and then carefully dived at the couch, and made it.

He didn't move. His eyes were open, but decidedly glassy.

Peg came out of the bedroom, rubbing her eyes. "Oh, bro-*ther!* Do I have to put *both* of you to bed?"

Anne picked herself up off the floor, laughing. "Nope. Just lend a hand with Junior here."

"Well," said Peg, "at least I don't get tossed out of my bed tonight."

"Hush," said Anne.

They went to work, trying to arrange two hundred pounds of inert mass. The inert two hundred pounds said, quite distinctly: "I am thoroughly capable of putting my own self in the sack." It said it twelve more times before they got him arranged on the couch and tossed a sheet over him.

"Night, baby," Anne said, and kissed him.

She undressed and went to sleep in the other room. She slept soundly as always. Once, very early in the morning, she thought she woke up and heard someone crying in the living room.

13

THE NEXT MORNING was on the miserable side, and by the time Ellery really began to sit up and take an interest in things, the girls had to go to work.

Ellery sat in the apartment and wondered what to do. Jefferson Springs sat there with him, smiling.

Last night, he had managed to shut out Jefferson Springs. He had stuffed it down into a back corner in his mind and poured alcohol on top of it. It had worked, too——

Except for the dreams.

"Damn it," he said. "Damn *me.*"

He wished, fervently, that he could forget all about Jefferson Springs, and forget everything that had happened there. He wished that he could simply unpack his bag where he was and never go back. He could go on and live a life, some kind of a life, and tell himself that it was none of his business. He didn't have to go on being a scientist; science was not a religion to him. He could just relax and persuade himself that a few facts didn't really matter. He would just say to himself, "I once knew a town less than two hundred miles from my

home, a town where people lived who thought of me as a
savage. I once knew such a town, but the hell with it."

He liked the idea.

Too bad that it was impossible.

Impossible for *him*. Paul Ellery had been cursed with a
mind that asked questions, looked for answers. His mind
worked whether he wanted it to or not, and he had never been
able to find the button that would turn it off. He had been
cursed with a stubborn streak a yard wide, and he had never
been broken. He had been cursed with a cynical soul that he
wasn't proud of; he had always thought that he should have
been better than he was, or at least dumber.

He could no more walk out of Jefferson Springs, licked,
than Cortez could have walked out of Mexico, or Columbus
could have quit before sighting land. It wasn't heroism, and it
wasn't noble. It was selfish pride, and he knew it.

Either he was going to beat Jefferson Springs or Jefferson
Springs was going to beat him. If he won, which he knew was
impossible, then he had done something for his people and
for himself. If *they* won, which was certain, then he would be
one of them, and he would have done something for himself.

Neat.

He wished he believed it in his guts instead of in his
head.

Okay, bright boy, he told himself. *You came up here to
think things out. Start thinking.*

The flash of illumination, the insight that would have
made the impossible easy, didn't come. Ellery paced the
floor, swearing diligently under his breath. He looked out the
window at the hot gray sky and cursed that explicitly. Why
didn't it rain?

He picked up the morning paper and stared at it glumly.

The same old crud. He read the story over, and a thought waded around below the surface and tried to be born.

He sat down, his head in his hands. He had three hours left before Anne came home. Three hours. Had he made any more progress, really, toward understanding what went on in Jefferson Springs? He told himself that he had not, and then he wasn't so sure.

For one thing, now that he thought about it, that ritual in the blue lights at the Thorne Ranch had told him plenty. It had given him a needed clue into the workings of the colony culture. If that was a prime source after the "full treatment," and if the citizens of the colony spent all or most of the rest of their time in living the lives of small-town Texans, then there was only one possible technique they could be following.

If all human beings in all their variety had to start with an almost identical skeleton——

Well, leave that for the moment.

Take that story in the paper about China. That was interesting, definitely. What *was* the attitude of the United States toward China? That depended. Which China did he mean—the one on the island or the one in China? Did he mean the official policy of the United States Government? Which administration—past, present, or future? Did he mean the individual states? Which ones? Did he mean the "man in the street?" Which man? What street?

That was interesting. That was another clue.

So—how about the alien culture? What was he up against there, and how could he come to terms with it? What was the attitude of the whole alien civilization toward its colonial policy? John had hinted of friction there, hadn't he? Wasn't that what the big conference was going to be about?

What did they think of savages who climbed up the ladder?

Had John told him the *whole* truth about Jefferson Springs?

Questions. Always questions. Find the right question and you get the right answer. Questions——

How about the aliens, the people? Were *they* all identical robots, thinking alike, speaking alike, looking alike? The little fat man, high above the Earth, reading bad science fiction with a persecution complex? Mel Thorne, running his ranch in the sun? A. Jeremiah Stubbs, sitting on the one story he could never send out to the A. P. wire?

Cynthia?

And how about the *billions* of others, out there beyond his imagination? No conflicts, no disagreements, no factions? Nothing that he could use, nothing that he could turn to his own advantage?

Well, leave *that* for the moment. But don't forget it.

Of course, the whole problem posed by Jefferson Springs was a problem in acculturation, a problem created by the contact of cultures. One culture was extremely advanced, so advanced that he could hardly do better than to catch tantalizing, unsatisfying hints as to its true nature. The other culture was his own.

Or had been.

There was the catch he had thought of before: there was no acculturation problem for the two *cultures* involved, since one of them wasn't even aware that the other existed. But there was acculturation for *him*. He knew.

He thought, again, of Two Bears.

What happened to men caught between two cultures? What happened to a savage when civilization reared its metallic head? Well, he could be killed, of course, either literally or spiritually. He might try his luck with a spear against a tank, or he might watch his people die and smile. He might make himself useful to the civilized men, might even go to school and become one of them. He might run away, if there was any place to go. What else might he do? Was there *anything*?

Maybe. Just maybe.

In spite of himself, Paul Ellery felt a growing excitement. He was a man again. He would go back. This time, he knew what he was looking for.

By the time Anne and Peg came home, Ellery had shaved and taken a shower and put on clean clothes. He even managed to stick a smile on his face that was almost as good as the genuine article.

"Whee!" said Peg, kicking off her shoes and rubbing her ankles. "He's *alive* again! I like you so much better that way, Paulsy. I mean I really do."

Ellery kissed each girl impartially. "I'll make some coffee," he said. "You all sit down and radiate."

"My," said Anne, obeying orders. "What are we supposed to radiate—gamma rays?"

She looked trim and provocative in a white blouse and dark skirt with a red silk handkerchief around her throat. Ellery kissed her again for good measure. "You radiate beauty, of course," he told her. "Maybe a bath would help, but right now you do the best you can."

"Wait until you see that different, mysterious me," she said. "I come on after five, or at least that's what it said in the glamour magazine. Right now I *do* stink a little. You feeling better, hon?"

"Wait and see," he said cryptically and went out to make the coffee.

He proved it to her, taking the rest of the night for a

demonstration. They didn't do anything spectacular, but when they were right they didn't have to do anything at all. They had something to eat at Dirty Bill's Drive-In, and then they just drove, outside of Austin, out in the hills.

There was beauty around Austin, an unsuspected beauty that waited patiently for someone to come out and look at it. It was not a sensational, color-postcard kind of beauty. It was a beauty that asked for a pair of seeing eyes.

There was a long, comfortable lake, made by a dam across the Colorado. There were low hills, blanketed in sweet-smelling cedar. There was empty farmland, rolling away into the shadows. They drank it in, and neither talked of it. Then he drove Anne home.

"Paul," said Anne, "will you ever come back for me?"

"I don't know," Ellery said, hating himself. "I hope so. I want to, Anne. Remember that."

"I wish I knew what had happened to you down there. You're different, Ell. It's not just another woman this time."

"No. Maybe I'm growing up."

"Don't grow away from me, Paul. We're not so young any more, and it's lonely sometimes. You need me, too."

"Yes. No one else would put up with me."

"Could I come and see you?"

"No, baby. I don't want you down there. Don't make me explain."

"I'm only human, Paul."

"That's enough. Don't say any more. Don't talk."

It was three o'clock when he took her home.

"Come back to me, Ell. I can help, whatever it is. I've always helped you, haven't I, Paul?"

"Always," he said. "You're my girl."

"You'll come back, Paul? Please say you'll come back."

"I'll try, Annie. That's all I can say."

"Okay, hon. Sorry I love you so much. 'Night."

"Good night, Annie."

He drove away, trying to ignore the knot in his stomach.

He stopped at the University and walked across the gray campus, deserted in the early morning hours. He walked to steady himself, to clear his head.

And he walked to remember.

The cold gray buildings that he knew so well were like a living past. He knew them all, from Waggoner Hall, where he had taken his first course in anthropology, to the Tower that housed the library. He even knew buildings that were no longer there, like old B Hall, now just a plot of grass.

And the old faces came back, laughing and crying and unconcerned.

An icy melancholy crept over him as he walked and his blood was cold in his veins. With an almost numbing shock, Paul Ellery began to understand that his problem was far more than it had appeared to be. All his life he had rejected, questioned, rebelled. Not altogether, of course, and perhaps mainly in his mind. Maybe, even, it went with his kind of mind. Maybe it was necessary, if he was ever to understand. But the fact remained that even this was not wholly his.

He was an outsider not to one culture, but to two.

He shook the feeling off and went back to his car. He got in and drove through the sleeping city, back out the San Antonio highway and on toward Jefferson Springs.

And all through the night he thought. He thought of the Osage, who had discovered oil on their reservation. . . .

14

SEPTEMBER HURRIED BY, trailing rain and a crispness in the morning air. The land turned green, hurriedly, and the cactus flowers bloomed. The hot afternoon sun blazed down recklessly, not knowing what month it was, and tried to suck the moisture from the ground. But the rains had come and the rivers flowed, and then, quite suddenly, it was October.

John sent the same two men to escort Ellery to the ship. One of them was still smoking a pipe, and Ellery got the distinct impression that it had not gone out since he had last seen him. They came for him while he was at work.

"We must be quick," the man with the pipe said. "The delegates are already aboard, and we have a lot of territory to cover before the conference."

"On my way," Ellery said, yanking a sheet from his typewriter and handing it to Mr. Stubbs. "Here's the story on the garden club."

A. Jeremiah Stubbs did not look up. He slowly extracted his big gold watch from its nest and examined it with marked distaste. He adjusted his green eye shade and hooked his fingers in his black vest. "Young cub," he said gloomily. "When I was your age——"

Ellery slapped him on the back, startling him to such an extent that he actually tilted his swivel chair a full inch from its usual position. "I'll bet you were a demon!" Ellery assured him. And then to the two men: "Let's go."

Time twisted back on itself and played a remembered scene again. There was the black Buick and the country road, and then there was the ten-foot globe. He sat on the same green couch on the same gray carpet, and there was the same faint smell of electricity in the air. The globe lifted through the golden sunlight, carrying him very high this time, and then the panel slid open and there was a glare of gentle yellow light.

He was back in the giant spaceship, floating over the Earth.

Back down the long polished corridor, and even as he walked he felt a new vibration in the ship. It was subdued, but it carried a hint of power that was beyond his comprehension. For the first time, he was on the ship while it was in flight. He knew a fleeting moment of terror. He pictured the massive silver tube of the ship standing on her tail and pointing her nose up and out, flashing into the abyss of space, leaving the Earth far behind her, a dot in the infinite, and then nothing, nothing at all——

He pulled himself together. The ship would only be circling the Earth, picking up representatives from the star colonies.

He laughed shortly. That was all. Just alien delegates. How strange it was, he thought, this endless adaptability of the human mind. . . .

Back to the heavy door set flush in the end of the

corridor, the door that swung open without a sound as he approached it. Back to the familiar room, the padded chairs, the cluttered desk.

And John.

The fat little man beamed. He chuckled, hugely, like Santa Claus. He got out his bottle of Scotch and poured out two glassfuls. *He's glad to see me,* Ellery thought, and he was grateful. *He's really glad to see ME.*

"Ellery, old man!" John exclaimed. "Welcome back to the den of the fat monsters!"

"Howdy, John," Paul Ellery said, taking his drink and sitting down. "Thanks for not forgetting me."

"Nothing, nothing at all," John said, tossing down half a glass of straight Scotch at a swallow. "Ah! The delicate glow of hot machine oil. I've missed you, Paul. You have no idea how deadly dull it is to have to sneak around and be mysterious all the time. Damn it, I hate mysteries! I'm a straightforward man. How do you like being an alien, son?"

Ellery hesitated. "I don't know," he said finally.

"Fine!" said John. "How was Austin?"

"Strange," Ellery said truthfully. "Strange, and rather wonderful. How the devil did you know I was in Austin?"

John shrugged, his bald dome gleaming above its fringe of hair. "Elementary, my dear Paul. Nothing omniscient about it at all. I left you in a state of shock, and the next day it was noticed that your car was missing. I know you pretty well, old man; and it wasn't hard to guess that you'd go home. As a matter of fact, it's easier to keep track of you out of the colony than in it."

"Meaning?"

John pulled out a big black cigar and stuck it in his mouth. "Follow your instincts, Paul. At its somewhat primitive level, your science doesn't much believe in instincts any more, but you follow 'em anyhow."

"You're hinting at something, John-boy. What?"

John ignored the question. "I want you to see the ship before the yak-yak starts. And I want you to meet Withrow. He's been in the same situation you're in, and you two should have a lot in common."

They started to walk, with John leading the way. Ellery could feel the ship sliding to stops and then easing into motion again.

Picking up passengers, around the Earth.

They walked until Ellery's legs ached. John plunged on like a plump, eager puppy, and he never seemed to tire. Ellery once had estimated the length of the ship at five hundred yards, but he decided now that he would have to revise his estimate upward.

Way upward.

What he saw was astonishing enough—astonishing in its vastness and in its cool, comfortable efficiency. But what he could only sense was more astonishing still: a million engineering problems solved and hidden under his feet, problems as yet unformulated in the world he had known. A million answers to questions that might never be asked. . . .

There were computers and planetwide survey graphs. There were acres of files on unbelievable subjects. There were libraries and compact weapons that could wipe out a world at a touch of a button. There were hospitals and galactic communications equipment, bewildering in its complexity.

But he saw only the simple stuff, the toys.

And there were men and women, more alert and intense than those he had known in Jefferson Springs, technicians and engineers, and men who had long ago made a science out of anthropology and psychology and sociology, and then had gone on to something else.

When he saw the navigation room, he caught his breath. Three-dimensional mock-ups of galactic sectors, with stars and planets and moons and asteroids moving frigidly in magnetic fields, a universe stuck in a glass cage. And when two of the technicians computed a driveline, a triangular segment of star systems blurred eerily, so that the eye could not follow it, and the three dimensions that Paul Ellery had lived with turned into—something else.

He not only knew, now, that this ship could go a long, long way, he *felt* it.

"Don't forget, Paul," John said, watching his eyes when they were alone together for a brief moment "they're just people. Take a jackass and give him an automobile, and he's still a jackass."

Just people. What was he trying to say? "This conference," Ellery said. "It's about colonial policy, right?"

"Check. Maybe that's too much of an inflated term, though. This is just one planet, son. Peanuts. Strictly peanuts."

"I've been wondering," Ellery said slowly. "I'm not sure I understand your part in all this. What are *your* views about Earth?"

John looked him right in the eye and didn't smile. "Me? Why, I'm absolutely non-political. I have no views. I leave thinking to the smart men."

"Oh," said Paul Ellery. *Damn liar,* he thought.

"And now," John said, "you get to meet Withrow. Come along."

Ellery moved his legs again and wondered when the numbness would go away. "Who's Withrow?"

"Well, he used to be a writer—quite a popular one, as a matter of fact. He got to poking around in a little town in Maine about six years ago, and we made him the same offer that was made to you. He took us up on it, and he's been to the Center, so now he's one of us. You can probably learn a lot from Withrow."

Ellery was intrigued. Maybe here at last was someone who could be closer to him than either of the two cultures, a man who had been in the same boat that he was in. Maybe——

I need a friend, he thought. *I need one in the worst way.*

They found Withrow in a scanning cube, studying. Ellery sized him up. He was a thin, confident man with iron-gray hair, perhaps forty years old. He had cold, flinty eyes. He nodded at John and introduced himself to Ellery.

"Paul," he said, extending a businesslike hand, "I've heard a lot about you. I'm Hamilton Withrow. I hope very much that I can be of some help to you; I know how confusing things can seem at first." He smiled.

"I'm sure we'll get along," Paul Ellery said.

"Mr. Withrow has consented to do us a favor," John said. "Since you can't understand our language as yet, Hamilton has kindly offered to stay with you during the conference and let you know what is going on. I'll be busy elsewhere, being a non-political person."

"That's mighty nice of you," Ellery said.

"Not at all," said Hamilton Withrow.

John left them, presumably to go back to his office.

"Strange man," observed Withrow.

"John? He seems like a pretty good guy."

Withrow shrugged and didn't pursue the subject. "You know, Paul," he said, "I was in exactly your position once. I know the difficulties you're going through. If I may say so, all your doubts will vanish utterly after a short time at the Center. Your old life—and I mean no offense by this—will seem an amusing childhood, and your old friends just fondly remembered children. We must learn to take the long view, Paul, the *long* view."

"I appreciate your advice, Mr. Withrow."

"Please! My name is Hamilton—or even Ham, if you prefer." He laughed.

Ellery laughed, dutifully.

The hours passed, and the great ship swam around the Earth, scooping up her passengers like fish from a shallow sea. In what was really a remarkably short time, Hamilton Withrow led Ellery to the conference room, where things were starting.

It was a long, low room, staggering in its immensity. It was filled to overflowing with the strangest people Ellery had ever seen.

There were Chinese, English, American, French. There were Africans, Danes, Brazilians, Poles, Swedes, Japanese. There were Filipinos, Swiss, Australians, Russians. There were Negroids, Whites, Mongoloids. There were rich men, poor men. Men in business suits and men who were half naked. Women with rings through their noses, women with rings in their lips, women with rings on their fingers.

But the strangeness was more than their diversity. The strangeness was in their *similarity.* They were all self-assured, sophisticated, well-behaved. Even a bit smug, perhaps. They had a tangible sense of belonging, an unconscious air of superiority, an aura of power.

The people were human, all right. If a man could apply strictly objective criteria, they were undoubtedly the most human people on Earth. But they were not human beings as Paul Ellery had known them. They were somehow different, somehow alien. Almost, they were the Cro-Magnons as seen by the Neanderthals.

"Look at them!" Withrow exclaimed, his cold eyes shining. "Aren't they splendid?"

Ellery hesitated. "Splendid" wasn't quite the word that he would have used, but he decided against saying so. "Remarkable, no doubt of that," he said.

There was a great deal of soft conversation, filled with buzzes and clicks, and Ellery couldn't understand a word of it.

"We can't speak to each other in our adopted Earth tongues, you know," Withrow told him. "Each group knows only its own local language. So, when we get together, we have to use the mother tongue."

"Oh," said Ellery, glancing at Withrow. "The mother tongue."

Hamilton Withrow, however, failed to notice the speculative look. He was thoroughly wrapped up in the conference, his thin body proud and alert. Occasionally, he exchanged words with someone he knew, speaking quite fluently in the clicks and buzzes of the alien language. Ellery began to feel uncomfortable.

The conference started.

Ellery was unable to fathom the rules of procedure. Small groups appeared to work together, examining documents and talking softly, and then the various different groups would compare notes. Periodically, and seemingly apart from the group arrangements, someone would address the convention. While he spoke, perhaps five or six of the delegates would pause and listen to him. This, too, seemed to be somehow prearranged.

On one wall, there was a large white square, bordered in some black metallic substance. As the conference wore on, colored lights flickered into life on the square. They arranged themselves into flowing patterns, and altered after each speech. From time to time, a small group would send someone over to check the pattern against a small black gadget that fitted into the hand, and when the checker went back to his group there would be a renewed flurry of activity.

To Ellery, the whole thing took on a hypnotic, lulling quality. Very important and all that, but a little removed. Withrow could not translate a fiftieth of what was said, and Ellery could not understand a fourth of what was translated.

He listened and did his best.

"All automatic, you know," Withrow said. "All the variables are integrated, and then the free-choice element is factored out and manipulated."

"Ummmm," said Ellery. *And don't put the bananas in the refrigerator!*

"He's saying, essentially, that we must be practical about this thing. He says that our colonial policy was not a choice, but a necessity. He says we should give the colonials a greater voice in galactic administration. He suggests that Earth will soon blow itself back a thousand years, and then we can safely bring in more colonists. He says we must think of our children, and of our children's children."

"I see," said Ellery.

"This one's a bit wild. He says that our whole solution to the problem of overpopulation is nothing more than sticking our head in the sand. He says he isn't any aborigine-lover, but just the same he thinks we're headed for trouble. He says we should resurvey the whole galactic colonial system. I wonder where he thinks *he* would go if we left all the planets for the savages! You can see how muddy his thinking is, Paul."

"Sure," said Ellery.

"The next speaker—see him, the one with the abominable haircut—is saying—well, he is saying—you see, it's about the relation of the Prime Force to the Quadrant—I mean—well, I'm afraid it's a bit over your head."

"Don't worry about it," Ellery said.

He listened, and the meeting seemed to go on endlessly. There was a great deal of bickering about local problems: the position of the colony in the galactic economy, the possible importation of luxury items into backward areas, the problem of fraternization with the local savages. Ellery just couldn't take it all in. He had to keep telling himself, over and over: *This is Earth they are talking about, this is—was—my home they are discussing, my people—*

The voice droned on in his ear: "This one is advocating more interference to maintain the status quo . . . this one wishes to send missionaries among the savages; that's a good one . . . this one thinks we should send all colony-born children back to the Center *before* the high-school ages . . . this one . . . this one . . . this one . . ."

After an eternity, it was over.

The pattern of lights on the board flowed, steadied, and stopped. The result was announced.

"Same old thing." Withrow yawned. "The galactic colonial policy is approved, and more attention is requested for local problems. Doesn't mean a thing, but it keeps the colonists happy."

Ellery looked at Withrow. Unbidden, an image came

into his mind. An image from many years ago, from high school. A boy who had come out for football during the last month of the season, when it was too late for him even to get in shape, and had thenceforth referred to himself as "one of the team."

"You can probably learn a lot from Withrow," John had said.

John was subtler than he looked.

"I appreciate your help, Hamilton," Ellery said.

He was exhausted, mentally and physically. He let Withrow lead him out of the conference room, and back to John's office. He was glad when Withrow left him alone; he simply didn't feel up to talking to the man.

John wasn't in. Ellery thought dimly that this might be a good time to pick up some secret information from John's desk, but he rejected the idea. He already had more information than he could possibly handle; he was flooded with a deluge of information. His problem, he knew, was never going to be solved by any remarkable item filched from a desk.

There were no magic formulae.

Ellery compromised by walking over to a wall couch, stretching out, and going to sleep in seconds. It was the only retreat he had left, and it was good to get away for a while.

John woke him up, hours later, and brought him a cup of hot coffee, which he drank thankfully. He was stiff and sore, and he felt thoroughly insignificant.

"Jefferson Springs," John said quietly. "Time to go home."

"Thanks, John. What do I owe you for the room?"

"Not much, my boy. Shall we settle for your grandmother's arm and the mortgage on the family homestead?"

"It's a deal."

John himself escorted him down the long corridor, walking with deceptive speed. "You know, Paul," the little fat man said, "you're just beginning to get an insight into the size of this mess. That whole conference you witnessed was classed as a strictly rural affair. Maybe it'll get one line in the Galactic Administration Report, and nobody'll even read it. It's a bit shocking at times—did you know that more than ninety-nine per cent of the civilized people of this galaxy do not know that the planet Earth exists? It's strictly specialized information."

Ellery started. *Ninety-nine percent did not know—* Well, how could they?

"Quite stupid," John said, shaking his head. "The conference didn't even have the guts to *mention* the real problem."

Ellery raised his eyebrows.

"There are the Others, you know. I believe you caught a glimpse of them at the little gathering on the Thorne Ranch?"

Ellery remembered. *The galaxy, with gossamer silver threads. Atoms of worlds. And something else. Something down in the corner, down dark in the corner.*

Had he screamed?

They came to the panel that led to the metallic sphere which Ellery was beginning to think of as an elevator.

"You'll be sent to a Center soon, Paul," John said. "Don't sleep too long."

Ellery stared at the fat man, waiting, but John said nothing more. The panel slid open and Ellery walked into the globe. He sat down on the same green couch, but this time it was more crowded. The two ship escorts were there, one of them still with his pipe in his mouth, and in addition there were the three conference delegates from Jefferson Springs, two men and a woman. The men wore boots and big hats, and the woman wore a black dress and a shawl. They sat next to him and made small talk, but the atmosphere was strained.

The great floating globe touched down, and they stepped out into a plowed field. It was night, and the blackness was frosted with stars. There was a cold moon, coating the Earth with silver. Ellery wasn't sure what night it was.

They got into the black Buick, and the car jolted over the dirt road, and then purred down the highway toward Jefferson Springs. Ellery sat in the back seat, crowded in with the three colonists. He didn't look at them and he avoided their eyes.

Too big, too big, he thought. *Too big to fight.*

He felt himself growing tense as the little town came closer. He sensed the vast bulk of the spaceship, lost in the stars over his head. He felt very small.

He couldn't beat them. Being what he was, he couldn't ignore them. After seeing Withrow, he wasn't even sure he could join them, and stay sane.

He thought about Anne, and wondered what she was doing.

He tried to think about Indians who had found oil on reservations.

He was very tired, and the big black Buick rushed on, into the shadows and the night and the pale splashes from an empty moon.

15

AUTUMN FLOWED SOFTLY by, easing its way toward winter. The land lost its brief flush of green and stood nakedly before the wind, but there would be no real freeze until January.

Paul Ellery kept digging, looking for the chink in the armor of Jefferson Springs. He knew that he was not learning fast enough, and he knew that it would not be long until they shipped him off to the Center for the "full treatment."

After that, he wouldn't care.

He saw Cynthia, occasionally, using her to fight the empty loneliness he felt in the town that was not his own.

Once, out walking on a country road, he spotted a piece of worked flint half buried in the dry, hard-packed earth. He picked it up and looked at it. It was a crudely made, pointed artifact about five inches long, bearing the characteristic flake scars of human workmanship. It was too long for an arrow point; it might have been a spear point, a dart point, or a stone knife. Probably not Comanche or Apache. Ellery wasn't certain, not being an archaeologist, but the flint had probably been used by one of the nameless hunting-and-gathering Indian groups that had been common throughout Texas before the beginnings of the written historical records.

Another way of life—vanished in the dust.

He stood in the chill wind and shivered.

The humble, long-overlooked bit of flint called forth a host of memories. He remembered the kick he had got out of his first anthropology courses. He remembered the long, all-night discussions, and the books that had seemed to open up wonderful, uncharted vistas of the mind—the excitement of Malinowski, the sweep and daring of White, the vision of Linton dedicating a work of social science to the next generation. He remembered his young confidence, his certainty that he had a key that would unlock doors that others could not see. And he remembered the subsequent plodding of graduate school, the hot digs, the quizzes on bone fragments, the wrestling with German. Fun, all of it; but what had happened to the excitement and the hope and the promise for the future?

When had it turned into uncertainty and caution and even fear? When had the kick in his work gone out the window?

Was it the apathy of his students? Was it the preoccupation with trivia of many of the scientists? Was it the discovery that social science had many questions but few answers?

Was it the flowering hell of the hydrogen bomb that reduced what he was trying to do to hopeless insignificance?

Was it a climate of cultural hysteria in which a scientist could not work?

Or had he failed himself, somewhere along the line?

He stood for a long time, the old artifact in his hand, and then walked back to town under the thin, pale sun.

He kept trying. And one day he found something.

It was late in the afternoon of a warm day. He stepped into the American Club for a beer. There was a little bell on the screen door, and it jingled as he walked through. The front room was furnished with four faded green pool tables and a few crooked wire stools. There were calendars on the walls, showing bathing beauties in love with Coca-Cola, cowboys in love with horses, and business executives in love with trout. There was a stained bar along one wall, made of plywood. There was no one in the room.

There were voices coming from the back room, behind a thin wood partition. Voices, and the click of dominoes.

He moved quietly over to the wall and stood with his ear pressed against it. He kept his eyes open. He could hear the voices clearly:

"I don't care what you say, dammit, the Administration is gonna throw us to the wolves."

Administration? That would be the galactic government.

"What're we supposed to do—just sit on our tails and let 'em take our homes away from us? You listen here to what I'm tellin' you boys——"

"Me, I say we oughta do more—a hell of a lot more! So maybe the Preventers are illegal—so what? They're workin' for *us*, and they're the only ones who give a good goddam about us."

Preventers? He had come across references to them before—an organization that believed in preventing a colonized planet from ever reaching civilized status, as opposed to the Evolutionaries who felt that colonized planets must be left alone to progress as best they could, without interference.

"Ahh, you take yourself too blamed serious. They'll blow their ratholes sky high without any help from us. Let the Preventers stick their necks out if they're a mind to. Me, I ain't forgettin' that ship up yonder, and don't *you* forget it neither. You remember what happened to that colony down south, don't yuh? Polio, they said——"

"They're a pack of damn Evolutionists in One Sector, if you want *my* opinion. I ask you, what do them jokers know about *practical* problems?"

"Take it easy, there, you're not yellin' into a tornado."

"Ahh, what're yuh scared of—the F.B.I.?"

Laughter.

"Yeah, the hell with it. Bill, what say to a couple more beers?"

The sound of a chair scraping the floor. Footsteps.

Ellery hurried across the room and out through the screen door. He had forgotten the little bell, and it tinkled as the door swung. He walked down the sidewalk, then crossed the street and entered a narrow alley. He stopped by a garbage can and listened.

Nothing.

He kept moving, back on Main Street, down the block to his car. He got in, backed into the street, and drove past the club. There was no excitement there. No one was in the front room. Either he hadn't been seen or else they didn't care.

He went home to get dressed for a date with Cynthia. While he dressed, he thought over what he had heard.

The pieces were beginning to fall into place a little.

If only he had more time. . . .

Evidently, the aliens had not been able to eliminate an old, old problem in the field of government. There was a marked conflict betwen basic administrative policy, set by the Galactic Administration, and the colonies actually living in the field. The basic policy was fair and even altruistic. The great spaceship was there to see that the hands-off policy was followed to the letter. Unfortunately, the ship couldn't be everywhere at once, and some colonists didn't think too highly of basic policy. They were human enough to think of themselves first and ethical questions later, if at all. If the Preventers could only prod the native planets into atomic wars that would blast the city reservations, then the colonies were safe from eventual interference.

Probably, the Administration could handle the Preventers. Ellery was sure that John and the rest knew all about them, and were quite competent to deal with the problem. For Ellery, the important fact was simply that the colonists were divided in their sentiments.

That could be helpful.

Cynthia picked him up at eight. He climbed into her blue Nash and gave her a kiss.

"Hi love," she said. "In a dancing mood?"

"More or less. But I'm getting old for that sort of thing."

"You're not old, Paul."

"I feel old," he said, and meant it.

"We'll see if we can't rejuvenate you."

"You're the doctor."

They pulled up in front of the Community Hall, which was a drab, barnlike structure rearing up out of a lot of bare ground and a few earnestly struggling blades of grass. Her arm in Ellery's, Cynthia swished up the cement walk, cool and aloof in an off-the-shoulder dress of green taffeta. Ellery didn't mind dancing, and the Community Hall struck him as genuinely quaint, but walking into a building full of colonists still made him nervous. It was not fear so much as it was awkwardness and a sense of uncertainty, much as he had felt as a child when he had been cajoled into performing in a grammar-school play before an audience of adults. He had, he recalled all too vividly, dropped his spear and tripped on his toga.

He hoped that the inevitable punch was spiked, but he knew that it wouldn't be.

They made their entrance. Cynthia took the frankly admiring glances of the men in stride, accepting them as her due, and she returned the critical looks from the older females with icy disdain. She held Ellery's arm tightly, possessively.

It seemed to take forever, but eventually the buzz of conversation picked up again and filled up the sudden hush.

The inside of the Community Hall easily fulfilled the promise of its unglittering exterior. Primarily, it was empty space. Along the sides were folding chairs, and upon the chairs were seated the old women of Jefferson Springs. There were two doors at the back of the Community Hall which led to a kitchen. Music was provided by a portable phonograph plugged into a light socket. The phonograph was manned mainly by the high-school crowd, who watched Cynthia with frank speculation. Ellery wondered what she taught the kiddies in home economics.

The records in the Community Hall were somewhat dated, which suited Ellery fine. There was a lot of Glenn Miller, a sprinkling of Harry James, and a minimum of trick novelty records produced for the moron market.

The music played: *On a Little Street in Singapore. At Last. Serenade in Blue.*

Ellery danced, or at least shuffled his feet around. Cynthia politely turned down men who tried to cut in on them, and she felt light and pleasant in his arms. Ellery tried to forget where he was and just enjoy himself. All things considered, he did rather well.

The Community Hall simply wasn't very alien. And the girl in his arms was a beautiful young woman.

Along about eleven o'clock, after too much sweet and fruity punch, one of the boys decided to liven things up a bit. He seemed to be a standard Jefferson Springs product, with huge, rawboned hands dangling out of a too-tight and unfamiliar blue suit, but he had a taste for an upbeat tempo in his music. He diligently plowed through the Community Hall record stacks and turned up a dozen instrumentals. He risked the wrath of the football coach—who wasn't visible at the moment—by lighting a cigarette with airy unconcern. Then he proceeded to play the records, one by one.

He started off with *In the Mood*, and the dance floor cleared as if by magic, Paul started to join the exodus, but Cynthia pulled him back.

"Come on, love," she urged, her face flushed. "Show your stuff."

Ellery did his best, reluctantly at first, but warming to his task as he danced. He had never been the best fast dancer in the world, jitterbugging being an art that he had mastered solely to save himself embarrassment, and it had been a long time since he had really had to work up a sweat on the dance floor.

Watching the few remaining dancers out of the corner of his eye, however, he began to feel better about the whole thing. Unsensational though he was, he was better than *they* were. They were going through the motions easily enough, but they weren't letting themselves go. They seemed slightly uneasy, like a group of wrestlers dancing the minuet.

So, he thought, *there's one thing I know more about than they do!*

The music went from *No-Name Jive*, with its hackneyed but effective tenor sax solo, to Harry James's old *Two O'Clock Jump*.

Paul Ellery and Cynthia were alone on the dance floor.

Ellery began to show off. He twirled Cynthia around like a top, and she loved the chance to show off her legs. Ellery really got with it, closing his eyes in pseudo-ecstasy, and contorting himself. Cynthia kept up with him, but by God he was the star of *this* show!

He strutted half the length of the floor, and then the record stopped.

He laughed, his heart thumping merrily.

Then he heard the applause. It came at him from all sides, waves of it. Jefferson Springs was impressed.

Even Cynthia was clapping.

Paul Ellery stopped laughing.

The applause ended, and there was a sudden silence. Conversations started up, a little too quickly, and someone went over to the phonograph and put on a slow record.

Ellery stood very still.

"Oh, Paul!" exclaimed Cynthia, breathing hard. "You were positively *unique!*"

"Shut up," said Ellery.

"Why what's wrong, Paul?" She was smiling.

"*Shut up.*" His voice was louder than he had intended.

Some of the old ladies were looking at him.

He heard a whisper: "Savage!"

Blindly, Paul Ellery pushed his way outside, out of the building, into the cool night air. He stood alone, leaning against the wall. His sweat chilled and he clenched his fists.

Fool! I did it, right there in the middle of them. I did it, and I was proud of myself!

An exhibition. An exhibition of primitive dancing.

She made me do it. Damn her soul, she knew what she was doing. She tricked me, showed me off like a smart animal.

Paul Ellery saw red.

He looked around him in the starlight and found two rocks, one for each hand. He gripped them tightly.

He started for the door, where Cynthia stood framed in the yellow light.

He moved through a red haze, step by step.

And then he stopped. The whisper stuck, stinging his ears: "*Savage!*"

He dropped the rocks, listening to them thud when they hit the ground. He stood still, trying to control himself. He stood there for a long time, until he was sure that he was calm.

He was going to show them something about savages.

He didn't have his pipe, so he settled for a cigarette. He lit it with a steady hand, and blew a smoke ring up into the still air. He breathed deeply.

Then, quite casually, he strolled back into the Community Hall. There were three men watching him closely, but he didn't even look at them. He went straight to Cynthia and took her hand. She tensed, first in fear and then in surprise.

Paul Ellery smiled pleasantly. "Come on, dear," he said softly. "Let's go home."

Her blue eyes widened. "So—soon?"

His smile widened. "Not afraid of *me*, are you, Cyn?"

She hesitated. "Of course not."

"Then let's go."

"All right," she said. "All right, Paul."

They went home, to the little house across from the high school. It was a long night, and Ellery never touched her.

By morning, there was a certain respect in Cynthia's eyes.

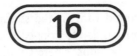

16

PAUL ELLERY KEPT DIGGING.

His job on *The Jefferson Springs Watchguard* didn't take up much of his time. He checked in almost every morning, typed up a story or two, and left. Mr. Stubbs handled the advertising, which was the biggest job on the paper, and how he did it was a mystery to Ellery. He never saw Stubbs move from his precisely tilted chair, and the old gentleman's eyes remained fixed on the blank wall, as though searching for impudent termites.

As a matter of fact, he supposed that Stubbs had his paper down to such a routine that it was virtually automatic. All of the accounts were handled by mail, and whenever anyone had a bit of news he always brought it in to Stubbs, like a faithful dog with a dead duck.

For a long time, Ellery had been puzzled by the absence of lights at night in Jefferson Springs. The town was never completely dark, except after midnight when everyone was asleep, but on the other hand it was never illuminated properly, either. The houses, particularly, were darker than they should have been. By eight or nine o'clock, there were seldom more than a dozen lights to be seen away from Main Street, and frequently there were none at all. In a town of six thousand, that didn't make sense.

The problem did not turn out to be unduly difficult to solve, once Ellery decided to investigate it. It was surprising, really, he thought, how many questions could be answered if only someone would go out and look. His method was simple, if unheroic. He became a Peeping Tom. He felt like an idiot, but he got his answer.

He spent two nights prowling through the dark streets of Jefferson Springs. He walked by houses first, to find out whether or not there was a dog around, and if he didn't draw any canine howls of fury he went back. The streets were poorly lighted, and except for passing cars, there wasn't enough light to pick him out. He just walked through the yard to the side of the house and looked through the windows. Or tried to.

All the windows had blinds over them, covering what was inside. The blinds were old-fashioned roller types, however, and he could usually find enough of a gap at the sides to look through. He saw very little at first, because the houses were dark, but he stuck with it, and eventually began to spot things.

A glimpse here, a hurried look there. The back of a head, a table, a shadowy figure.

And the blue lights.

Many of the houses were empty, but whenever he found one with people in it he found the blue lights with them. They were simple blue bulbs, as far as he could see, which were screwed into ordinary sockets. They gave off a pale blue light, identical with the blue light he had seen before, that night at the Thorne Ranch.

Around the blue lights were seated the people of Jefferson Springs, ten or more to each occupied house. They sat very still, in chairs or on the floor, and they never spoke. Their eyes were open—he could see them glinting dully in the eerie light—but they were fixed and unseeing.

Ellery listened closely, but he could not hear a sound. If there were any transmitters in operation, they were very quiet.

He never saw one of the meetings start, because they began early and he was afraid to risk sneaking around while it was still light. He did see two of them break up. At an invisible signal—evidently a time lapse of some sort, since it hit them all at the same moment—the people came out of their trances. The host turned off the blue lights and replaced them with plain white light bulbs. There was coffee and casual talk, and then the visitors went back to their own homes.

Ellery stayed hidden. As long as he was careful (and didn't leave town) no one would spot him. The colonists were not omnipotent.

He had enough data now to make some sense out of what he saw. Clearly, the colonists took turns acting as hosts for small groups of people; one night at one house, the next night at another. The blue lights had been used at the community ritual at the Thorne Ranch, and evidently these smaller gatherings served much the same purpose. They were ceremonies, ceremonies with a distinct religious flavor.

How did they work? There was no talk, and no apparatus that Ellery could see. The people just sat down, the blue lights went on, and the people entered into a state of trance. What happened then? Well, the colonists must have been conditioned in such a manner that they could go into a kind of direct voluntary hypnosis by looking into the pale blue lights. Something more than hypnosis, probably, but certainly related to it. What did it accomplish? Ellery was certain that it served to open their minds to some form of suggestion that had been previously implanted in them. Sitting there in the blue lights, they looked at nothing. And they saw——.

Who could say? Scenes and events and commands that tied them to the larger whole of which they were a part, experiences that Paul Ellery could only guess at. Experiences he could never know, until he went to the Center.

That was what Centers were for.

The citizens of Jefferson Springs. Watching scenes undreamed of on Earth.

Back in *his* house. Ellery sat alone at the kitchen table and wondered about Cynthia. She, for one, passed up a lot of rituals. Perhaps she wasn't a good citizen. But she had gone to one ceremony, and she had done her bit.

Ellery was making progress. He knew that, and felt a certain satisfaction in it. But he knew, too, that he wasn't making progress fast enough. Still——

He had the key to the alien culture now. His notebook was paying off. His notebook and the long, lonely hours. He had the key.

What made it possible for members of a galactic civilization to live in a primitive culture? How could they possibly spend their lives going through the motions of what was, to them, an alien life? How did the galactic colonial system *work?*

It wasn't a masquerade. That was the first thing to remember. These people, up to a certain point, believed in the lives they were living. These were their lives, and this was their culture. It had to be.

But it wasn't their *only* culture. That was the catch.

What the galactic administration had done was to indoctrinate its colonists with a hard core of civilized premises and beliefs. That was the skeleton, the same for every citizen, no matter where he might live. On top of that core of culture, the administration had grafted the customs and habits of the area to which the colonist was to be sent. That was the face and flesh and fingerprints, different for every citizen as it was for every human being.

It took some doing, of course. There was plenty of opposition. The whole scheme would have been utterly impossible in an uncivilized society. That, however, was just the point: these people were civilized.

They had learned, long ago, that it was the cultural core that counted—the deep and underlying spirit and belief and knowledge, the tone and essence of living. Once you had that, the rest was window dressing. Not only that, but the rest, the cultural superstructure, *was relatively equal in all societies.*

Human beings, by virtue of being human beings, had certain structural "musts" that had to find outlets. They had to eat and sleep and mate. All societies provided for such needs. And if you were conditioned to live in one specific society, you did it in the way the society specified, and you liked it—because that was your way, too. Beyond those basic needs, all cultures provided systems of handling the products of group living. Families? They could be monogamous or polygamous, matrilineal or patrilineal. You liked the one you were brought up in. Economy? It might be hunting or fishing or raising crops or buying food in a can. You liked what you were used to. The arts? They might include beating on a log drum, dancing in masks, or reading books. You were pleased by what you had been trained to like.

The colonists had the core. Beyond that, they could be taught to live with any cultural trapping—*and they could be happy in any society in which human beings could be happy.*

The core of civilized culture was reinforced and kept alive by community rituals that maintained contact with the mother culture. The techniques varied from society to society, but the purpose was always the same, and it worked, within human limits. It worked because the galactic administration knew what it was doing. It worked because the civilization involved had learned enough to pull it off.

It worked, too, because the really intelligent and successul citizens attained responsible positions in their native cutures. In a word, they stayed home, or worked in the Galactic Fleet. The ones who were farmed out to the colonies as population overflow were the weak and the dull and the uncaring—and the misfits. That wasn't the way it was planned, but that was the way it worked.

Adults were conditioned in the Centers before they were permitted to move into colonies. Children who were born in the colonies were indoctrinated by the colonies at the same time that they received instruction in the culture in which they found themselves and then before maturity they were sent "home" for intensive training and conditioning for a period of three Earth-years.

Paul Ellery had the key to the alien culture. He understood it as well as any outsider could ever hope to understand it.

But what could he do with his key?

How could he *use* it?

He didn't know.

And so he went on, doing the best he could, while time ran out on him. He was convinced now that he wasn't going to *find* any secret weapon that would turn defeat into victory. He didn't give up, but he did reaffirm his earlier decision.

He did it, oddly enough, at a football game. It was the last one of the season, and it was played on Thanksgiving. Jefferson Springs was playing Eagle Pass. The game was played at night, as always, under the lights. This was because the merchants were all busy on Saturday or holiday afternoons, when the ranchers came to town; and the games drew bigger crowds at night.

Ellery went with Cynthia, who looked fresh and young and almost innocent in skirt and sweater and loafers. He had a good seat and he enjoyed the game. Texas high-school football was rough, tough, and fast. It was played for blood. The fields were apt to be pitted and rock-strewn, the bands were customarily out of tune, and the pep squads were more strident than effective. But the games were good and hard and well played.

Cynthia watched with complete detachment, although she uttered the correct noises at the proper times. Ellery, who had been under the lights himself a long time ago, was quieter than he should have been, because he was rooting for the wrong team. He was pulling, desperately, for Eagle Pass.

They had two brothers, Dave and Tom Toney, at quarterback and halfback. They were good, giving all they had and then some, and Ellery cheered them silently.

Come on, Dave, he thought, *come on Tom. Sock it to 'em!*

Dave and Tom socked it.

Ellery felt a thrill of pride. The Jefferson Springs boys played earnestly, but they lacked the sparkle. They felt a bit superior, and that was deadly. Eagle Pass surprised them, with a bruising line and a tricky backfield.

Come on Dave, come on Tom!

The lights on the towers soaked the field and hid the

stars. The creaky wooden grandstands swayed whenever the fans stood up and hollered. The referee blew his whistle, and the yardage chain moved up and down the sidelines, following the ball.

Ellery kept his fingers crossed. He was still an outsider. He didn't belong to Jefferson Springs. He didn't even belong to Eagle Pass, but he felt closer to them. They, at least, had been his kind.

Ellery watched the field and wrestled with his thoughts. He decided, again, what he had to do.

Sock it to 'em!

He could not go on living a life without meaning. He could not go back to Anne and live a life in a zoo. He could not bring children into a world in which they would live on a reservation, devoting their lives to finding out things already a million years forgotten by others, facing a frightful future in which cities disappeared in a searing flash.

There was no secret weapon that he could find. The galactic set-up was simply too prodigious to be overthrown by one man, and particularly not by an ignorant savage.

He would keep trying, yes, because he had to. But if he could not come up with a real solution to his problem by the time the aliens decided to send him to the Center, there was just one thing to do. He would go to the Center and make no fuss about it.

After that, he wouldn't be Paul Ellery any more.

Come on Dave, come on Tom!

Now that it was lost to him, his world looked pretty good. He thought of it, with all its laughter and sadness and beauty and squalor, and he wanted it. He wanted it very much.

But not a world without purpose or meaning. Life was too tough if it was all for nothing.

Maybe he wouldn't have to be another Hamilton Withrow—Withrow, probably, hadn't been any prize specimen even before the "full treatment." Maybe he could even be another John. He liked John. It would be better than the life he was living now—tolerated, but not a part of things. Any culture was better than none, if you believed in it. And he *would* believe in it, after the Center. No doubt about that.

Attaboy, Dave! Attaway, Tom!

Eagle Pass won, and whooped jubilantly off the field. It was Thanksgiving, and in his own way Ellery give thanks. He was proud of his boys.

Dammit, there must be *some* way! If only he had more time . . .

Someone tapped him on the shoulder as he stood up. He turned around. It was Samuel Cartwright, portly and with his pink face gleaming with shaving lotion. The mayor of Jefferson Springs.

"'Lo, Cynthia," he said, with just the trace of a lisp in his speech. "Good to see you, Paul. How are you getting along?"

"Fine," lied Paul Ellery. "I'm getting along fine."

"Mighty good," said Mayor Cartwright. "I'm happy to hear that. By the way, Paul——"

"Yes?"

"I wonder if you'd drop around to my office tomorrow—you know where it is, over in the Court House. I'd like to talk to you a bit."

"What about?"

"Oh, a few plans for your future, and things like that. It's important that you be there, Paul. You know."

"I know," said Paul Ellery, his heart sinking. "I'll be there."

"Fine," said Mayor Cartwright. "I'm sure our talk will be satisfactory."

Cynthia smiled.

17

THE JEFFERSON SPRINGS Court House stood alone, its brick arms outstretched to try to cover a city block. It was a relatively modern-looking structure, and it had an air of distinct surprise about it, as though it still had not recovered from the shock of finding itself in Jefferson Springs. It stood on a side street, just across from the water tower. It was surrounded by elderly gentlemen engaged in an endless contest to determine the best and most consistent expectorator in Jefferson Springs.

Mayor Cartwright perched in haughty aloofness in an office on the second floor. To prove with crushing conclusiveness that he was a politician not to be ignored, he had both a water cooler and an open box of cigars in his office.

Paul Ellery waited until almost ten to give the great man plenty of time to settle himself in his sanctum, and then knocked on his door.

"Come in, come in!" urged the Mayor, in his best never-too-busy-for-my-constituents voice.

Ellery went in.

Samuel Cartwright shook his hand and offered him a

cigar. Ellery took it, out of politeness, although he was not overly fond of cigars.

"Close the door, Paul. That's the spirit. Now sit down, take a load off your feet. There. Nice day, mighty nice."

"Powerful nice," Ellery said.

"Yes, sir. Go on Paul—light up that old cigar! I like to see a man comfortable. No airs in *my* office, son. I'm a plain man."

Everbody calls me "son," thought Ellery. *What kind of biology do they have where they come from?*

Mayor Cartwright flicked on a lighter that actually worked, no doubt a product of alien super-science, and set Ellery's cigar on fire.

"Thank you," said Ellery, and blew out a big cloud of smoke to prove that he was enjoying the cigar.

"You're mighty welcome, Paul. Now we can get down to business. I reckon you know why you're here, Paul."

"More or less. I hope I haven't done anything wrong?"

"Not at all, son, not at all. Your conduct, if I may say so, has been exemplary."

True blue, that's me. "Nice of you to say so, Mayor."

"I know it hasn't been easy for you, Paul," the Mayor said slowly, speaking carefully to avoid his lisp. "You've been with us now for almost six months, and you've been in a difficult position. It isn't easy for a man to throw away his old life and start in on a new one. All of us know that, Paul. We've been through it ourselves."

"I guess you have, at that."

"We surely have. We've been watching you, and you've handled yourself very well. However, we have found it advisable not to prolong the adjustment any longer than necessary. A man can't do it all by himself. There comes a time when he needs help. There comes a time when he has to get off the beach and swim in deep water."

"You're right, of course," said Ellery.

Cartwright puffed on his cigar. "That's what the Center is for, Paul. It's to help *you*. We want you to understand that. We ourelves have had to go through Centers, and we send our own children to them. It will take a few years, and there is a certain discipline that you will have to put up with, but in the long view it's all for the best."

"When do I start?"

"As it happens, there will be a convoy ship in this area very early on the first of January—about one o'clock in the morning, I believe. You'll be picked up in a sphere just outside of town, on Jim Walls's ranch. After that, you'll be under Center jurisdiction until they judge that you're ready to come back and take your place in society. I'm fairly sure that you'll be assigned to Earth, since you are already familiar with the customs and the language here, but of course that will be up to them. You'll be leaving on New Year's Day, actually." He smiled proudly. "Rather a nice touch of symbolism, I think."

"Very nice."

"You'll see things and experience things and learn things that are beyond your imagination, Paul. It will be more than a whole new world—it will be a whole new *universe*. And when you come back, you'll be one of us—really one of us. You will have to take my word for the fact that when you come back, Jefferson Springs will seem very different to you. You have barely seen the surface here, Paul. When you return your real life will begin."

"I understand that."

"I'm sure you do. And Paul——"

"Yes?"

"When you come back, you will of course be under our laws—or the laws of some other colony. You may have observed that they can be rather strict under some circumstances. I'm not threatening you, understand; the necessity for our laws will be impressed upon you at the Center. I'm sure that you can see that our position requires diligent law enforcement. This is, you realize, as much for the protection of the natives as for our own safeguarding. Until you leave here, you are legally classed as a native, if you'll excuse my frankness, and you are protected under our laws. We have taken pains to explain your legal position to you previously. If you have any intention of changing your mind about taking advantage of our offer, Paul, now's the time to do it. You can leave now, and still be under Administration protection as a native of Earth. But it will be too late once you board the Center ship, and when you come back you will not, of course, be quite the—same."

"I've made up my mind," said Ellery.

"Fine. Mighty fine. I'm sure everything will go smoothly for you. Until the ship picks you up, just keep right on at your job, and I hope that things will not be unpleasant for you."

"You've all been very kind."

"Well, we *try* to do the decent thing, Paul. We really do. Our position here has its own difficulties, and we take considerable pains, if I may say so, to conduct ourselves like civilized men and women."

"I appreciate it."

"All right, Paul. I'll probably see you again before you leave. The best of luck to you."

He shook Ellery's hand again, and Ellery left the Court House. When Ellery was safely away from both the building and the spitters, he carefully took the cigar from his mouth and ground it under his heel.

Well, now he knew

He had a little over a month left. Thirty-odd days to be Paul Ellery.

It would be very easy to give up and take what was coming. He could almost do it now. A man could butt his head against a stone wall for only so long, and then he discovered that the wall wasn't going to come down.

He endured some chili and crackers at the Jefferson Springs Cafe, risking a volcanic eruption in his stomach, and then he went to work.

It was one in the afternoon when he checked into his office. Abner Jeremiah Stubbs placed both feet firmly on the plank floor and hauled out his big gold watch. He examined it distastefully, replaced it, and adjusted his green eye shade.

"Official business," Ellery explained. "I had to see the Mayor."

"You had to see the Mayor," Mr. Stubbs repeated, placing each word under a mental microscope. "You—had—to—see—the—Mayor."

"You've got the essence of it, Abner."

"My name, young man, is *Mister* Stubbs."

"But your friends call you Abner, isn't that right? Well, am I or am I not your friend? Now I'll get to work and write your front page for you. We can go to press early tomorrow."

"Well," said Mr. Stubbs, pleased. "Getting ink in your veins, eh son? I knew you had the makings of a newspaper man."

"Thank you, Abner," said Ellery.

He proceeded back to his office and heard the creak of the chair which indicated that Mr. Stubbs had resumed his customary tilt and had engaged his attention with the opposite wall. Ellery forced open the window, which seemed to close itself by magic every night. It was getting a little chilly, but the room was too stuffy to work in with all the windows shut.

He sat down before his venerable typewriter, stuck in a yellow sheet, and went to work.

One month to go.

HOME TALENT RODEO PLANNED.

Would Cynthia be waiting for him, if he came back? Did he *want* her to be?

NELLIE FAYE MOSELY WEDS BILLY JOE ADAMS IN CHURCH SERVICE.

Who were the Others? Where were they, what were they like, what did they have to do with all this? Why had he screamed when he had sensed them that night?

LOVELY PARTY IS COMPLIMENT TO CARRIE SUE ROBERTS.

What was John's role in all this? He had more than one, Ellery was certain, but *what were they?*

The phone rang. His phone. It was an ancient instrument in the corner, and he could not reach it from where he sat. It *never* rang. Ellery hadn't even been positive the thing was connected.

He got up and answered it.

"Yes?"

"Mr. Paul Ellery?"

"Speaking."

"We have a long-distance call for you from Austin, Texas. Hold the line please."

Ellery fumbled for a chair and sat down. Austin——

"Hello. Paul? Paul, is that you?"

Anne. His hand began to sweat.

"Yes, Annie. This is me."

"Paul, what on earth are you doing in a newspaper office? I called information and they said that's where you'd be. Paul, what are you doing?"

Mr. Stubbs's chair squeaked in the other room.

"I can't explain just now, Annie. But I'm okay. Don't worry."

"Paul, you sound so far away! Ell, this is Annie."

"I know, hon. It's hard to talk right now."

"Ell, I want to see you. I've got to see you."

"I want to see you, too, Annie. You know I do."

"I don't mean to be nosey, baby, but you haven't written or phoned or anything. Have you gotten my letters?"

"Yes. Yes, I've gotten them."

"Paul, I know it's none of my business. But it's been so long! You know I've tried never to bother you—but—but we've been so close—and I thought——"

"Yes, Annie."

"Ell, could I come down? Just for a little while? I know you must be busy and everything, but I could catch the bus here—I could come Friday and maybe we could drive back together—that isn't asking very much, is it Paul?"

"No, hon. It isn't asking anything at all."

"Can I come? Shall I come? I hate to be so silly——"

"Annie."

"What?"

"Annie, you can't come here."

"Paul, what's *wrong?*"

"I can't explain, I just can't."

"My gosh, you don't have to be so *mysterious* about everything! You talk like you were phoning from Dracula's castle or something. Why *can't* I come down?"

"You just can't, baby. If I could tell you why, I would."

"You—you mean you don't *want* me to come. Is that it, Paul?"

Ellery felt the floor spinning under him. *Go ahead, damn you*, he told himself. *Go ahead and act as if you don't care. Make her hate you. It's the only thing you can do for her now. Be decent for once in your life. Think of somebody else, just once.*

"Is that it, Paul?"

"Yes, Annie," he said. "I'm afraid that's it."

Silence. A silence that rocked the room.

"Paul?"

"Yes, Annie."

"I loved you, Paul. I really loved you."

She hung up. The *click* in his ear sounded like an explosion.

Ellery slowly put the receiver back on the hook. He went over and took the yellow paper out of his typewriter. He gathered up his stories, and handed them to Mr. Stubbs, who was standing in the doorway.

"Easy does it, Paul," Mr. Stubbs said softly.

"Thanks, Abner."

He hurried outside to a pale afternoon sun. He walked fast, away from the office, not going anywhere special.

Just walking.

His eyes were stinging in the chilly air, and it was hard for him to see.

18

FOR PAUL ELLERY, time ticked itself out.

The days between Thanksgiving and Christmas had always gone fast for him. He could remember, in school, that the two holidays seemed to come so close together that they almost merged into one. He had never thought much about Christmas coming at the end of the year. It was just a needed break in the routine of classwork, a pleasant time of friendship and relaxation, and then before you knew it New Year's Eve had come again.

New Year's Eve was a party night. It was a night he had spent with Annie for—how long now?

A night of champagne, a night of laughs.

A night of auld lang syne.

A night of fun.

He had never really thought of it as the end of a year. To be sure, he had to remind himself to change a numeral when he was dating letters, but that was about all. He had always religiously skipped the tired editorials and the unfunny radio comedies about New Year's resolutions.

But now it was ending. An ending of his life, and of the Paul Ellery he had known.

It had been a chill, rainy December, and now it was Christmas Eve. Seven days left.

He had worked at his notebooks, half-heartedly, but he wasn't getting anywhere. The secret weapon stayed a secret. More likely, it wasn't even there.

It was seven o'clock in the evening—a nothing hour that was like the phrase someone had coined about the countryside between the cities, an hour that seemed to be designed as a gap between something and something else. It was already dark in Jefferson Springs, and there was little to indicate that it was an evening different from other evenings. Jefferson Springs hadn't even bothered to string up the colored lights and paper bells with which other small Texas towns tried to hide the fact that it almost never snowed in their part of the country.

Ellery had hoped that Cynthia would call, but she was busy somewhere else. He was pretty damned lonesome, and he didn't know what he could do about it.

He didn't have any presents, because they had all been sent to his home. He didn't even think about going home. Somehow, childishly, he missed his presents. He felt forgotten. He knew that it was strictly his own choice, but that didn't help much.

He did have a radio, and he let it play, just for the hell of it. He heard Santa Claus. Santa, it seemed, was spending Christmas Eve in front of the Alamo in San Antonio, and was sponsored this year by a big department store.

Ellery tried another station.

This time he got Christmas carols. They had a sort of melancholy beauty, but they depressed him terribly. He tried again, and suffered through a drama about a mean old man who was just pure gold way down deep, especially when he heard bells and smelled turkey, and whose crusty manner concealed a deep-rooted and decidedly senile sentimentality toward all small children, all homeless dogs, and certain selected cats.

At eight-thirty, there was a knock on his door.

He got up, hoping that it was Cynthia, and swung the door open. It wasn't Cynthia. Instead, like a scene from an old play, it was the two men who had twice escorted him to the great spaceship that hovered over the Earth. The only difference was that this time the perpetual pipesmoker was not smoking.

"Well, gentlemen," Ellery said, glad to see anybody, "won't you come in?"

They hesitated. "We brought you a note," said the one who didn't smoke a pipe.

"Come in anyhow," Ellery insisted. "You know, I must be an awful lot of trouble for you two."

They smiled, almost bashfully. "Not at all," said the pipesmoker. They came in, a bit reluctantly, and sat down on the couch. Ellery took his message, an ordinary white envelope, and tore it open. There was a single sheet of paper inside, with a typed note on it:

"Christmas Eve is no time to be alone. The Scotch is ready. Come on up and we can cuss out Withrow. John."

Ellery felt better. Much better.

"You know," he said to the two men, "I don't even know your names."

The pipesmoker said: "I'm Bob. He's Clark."

Maybe their specialty isn't conversation. "How about some wine, before we go back? Bob? Clark?"

"No thanks," said Clark. "We're on duty, you know."

"Thanks anyway," said Bob. "We're still working our way up, and that sort of thing can lead to trouble."

"Okay," said Ellery. "You know best."

He turned off the radio without regret, and switched on the porch light. After that, the journey was like the others. They got in the big black Buick—did the car stay out in the fields between trips, or what?—and drove out of town. This time the metallic sphere was resting on the Walls Ranch just outside of town. The thing was almost invisible, actually; even when you knew it was there, you could hardly see it until you were almost on top of it. They entered through the panel, and the elevator lifted, buoyantly, up into the night.

Ellery did get one piece of information out of the two men. Bob had fired up his pipe again, with an almost audible sigh of relief. Feeling expansive, he said: "You know, you're quite exceptional, Mr. Ellery."

"How do you mean?"

"I've never seen the old man take such an interest in one of the—in one of the——"

"Natives," supplied Ellery, smiling.

"Yes. Pardon me, I meant no offense."

"Forget it. Facts are facts."

Bob nodded, admiringly. "The old man is—hard to get to know," he said. "He must like you."

Clark nudged his companion, and Bob said nothing more. Ellery gathered that dealing with the natives was apt to be a tricky sort of business. As a general rule, no doubt, it was left to trained contact men like John. Ellery hoped that he wasn't just part of a day's work for John, but it was hard to tell.

Still, there *did* seem to be something more at stake, even

though he was unsure as to what it was. John did his job, of course, but that wasn't *all* he did.

Well, if John had something up his sleeve he would have to shake it out this time. Paul Ellery wasn't going to be around much longer.

The globe hummed into the invisible ship and stopped. There was a muffled thump as it locked into place. The sliding panel opened, and the yellowish ship light flowed in.

The two men stood aside and let Ellery find his own way. He walked through the interlocking passage and into the long hallway with the closed panels. He walked down its spotless length, the vast ship throbbing ever so slightly around him, and stepped toward the heavy door set flush with the wall. The door opened without a sound, and Paul Ellery walked into John's sanctum.

The little fat man was seated behind his desk, his feet propped on a spare chair, reading a magazine. He looked up eagerly, and slammed the magazine down with a gesture of supreme irritation.

"Propaganda, that's what it is," he snorted. "Propaganda! Paul, I'm glad you could come. Damn glad!"

"Thanks," said Ellery, warming to the man's bursting personality. He shook his hand, firmly. "It was very kind of you to ask me to come."

"*Nonsense,* Paul. Nonsense and garbage! Don't you think *I* ever get lonesome up here?"

"Well," said Ellery, sitting down in the chair in front of the desk, "you have your job, your friends, all that."

"My friends are muttonheads," announced John. "I seem to recall that you like Scotch, so I've requisitioned a new supply. It's quite good, really, for a primitive drink. Got a kick to it, a little of the old *sock*. We're getting soft, sophisticated. Ought to get back to fundamentals."

He poured out two drinks, downed his own at once, and poured himself another one.

Ellery felt himself relaxing, forgetting his troubles. *Therapy*, he thought. *John's a pretty fair country doctor.*

"I see you're reading science fiction again," Ellery said, indicating the crushed magazine on John's desk.

John leaped at the bait, eagerly.

"Incredible," muttered the fat man indignantly. "Absolutely fascinating at its best, but so fantastically far off the beam so much of the time."

John polished off his second Scotch. Ellery, knowing John of old, fished out his pipe, lit it, and settled back for the deluge. But even as he settled back, he thought: *He brought me here for a reason. This is his last chance. If he's ever going to do anything, it will have to be now.*

John, however, seemed splendidly unaware of the role he was supposed to play. He was off on his pet peeve. He surged to his feet, bristling, and picked up the science-fiction magazine.

"Look at that," he ordered, holding up the cover. "*Look at that.*"

Ellery looked, without much interest, humoring his host. The cover portrayed a bald gentleman with a swollen head. The bald gentleman was staring intently at a wrench, which was hanging in the air, fastening a bolt.

"You *see*?" demanded John.

"Well," said Ellery, "what is it?"

"It's a superman, dammit!" John exclaimed. "I *hate* supermen!"

The fat little man with the red face took another hefty

pull at the Scotch and began to pace up and down his office. There was something compelling about the man, something dynamic, something that held your attention riveted to him. He held you, even when he was off on one of his crazy tangents, even when your mind was watching in amazed wonder, asking——

Why?

"You hate supermen," Ellery said. When at a loss for words of your own, he had long ago decided, you could always repeat the other fellow's. He tried to keep his voice matter-of-fact, but as far as he was concerned he might just as well have said, "You hate manhole covers." "Go on from there."

"Yes. Where was I? Ah, yes. Now, I'm a fair-minded man. I would be the last to condemn a craftsman for failing to incorporate in his work data that were unknown at the time he wrote. You wouldn't yell at Shakespeare because he didn't write a story about the hydrogen bomb, would you?"

"No, I wouldn't."

Ellery watched the little man—earnest, red-faced, pot-bellied, a fringe of hair girdling his balding head. John was a bundle of paradoxes. He was a man out of the future, but he resembled nothing so much as a jovial monk or friar from the Earth of long ago. He was frantic and incredible, but he was genuine. He kept out of reach, tossing around ideas that were irrelevant beyond belief, and yet he was communicating something, something that had to be said.

"You look here," John said, waving the magazine. "I don't mind when writers get to yakking about ridiculous mutations that take place without benefit of genetics, that just happen in the 'germ plasm' every time an atom bomb cuts loose. I don't mind when they blithely blow up whole planets filled with intelligent life just to keep the story going. I don't mind racial memories and Atlantis and *psi* factors. I don't mind when they portray everything in outer space as a ghastly monster. I don't object at all when I am depicted as a fiend, damn them. I *do* mind their confounded mutant supermen who take the normal, mixed-up kiddies by the hand and lead them forward to the promised land. Supermen *stink*."

"Oh?"

"A profound observation. Look here, Paul. You're supposed to be a scientist, right?"

"I was, yes."

"You are, yes. Now, if that brain of yours has not atrophied from lack of use, what do you think about a theory that postulates that man progresses because his brain gets bigger and better? Do you think that the next great advance of mankind will come about because of some mutant superman who points the way ahead, like Og, Son of Fire?"

Ellery considered, puffing on his pipe. "I think the theory's wrong," he said.

John sat down in sheer exasperation. "Listen, Paul," he said, "you *know* that theory is wrong. You want some proof?"

"Sure."

John stood up again. "*I'm* proof. Confound it, man, do I have to hit you over the head with it? I represent a civilization as far superior to yours as yours is to the Cro-Magnons'. Here I am, Paul! Am I a superman? Hardly. Am I in any physical way superior to you? Absurd—you could demolish me with one swat. And I *assure* you I cannot read your mind, and have not the slightest desire to do so."

"Okay, John, but what's——"

"Don't rush me." John sat down again, and helped himself to the Scotch. "I'm going to tell you a story. You already know it, but I'll tell it anyhow. On this planet called Earth, a very old but never tiresome story is in progress. Its hero is an animal called man. We'll just dispense with all man's fore-runners here—I'm talking about H. Sapiens, Esquire. Call him Cro-Magnon when we first look in on him; it's as good a name as any. There he is, living in caves, existing as a big-game hunter. *His brain is as good as yours, or mine.* Now, let's take a snapshot here and there, at long intervals. Our hero discovers agriculture. He becomes a food producer. His small village expands. A more complex technology develops, and specialists appear, and new kinds of social organization. Man has an Industrial Revolution. He lives in cities, a fact which we have utilized to our own advantage. He splits the atom, a fact which may also be utilized to our advantage. That is the first chapter of the story, Paul. The rest of the book has yet to unfold here on Earth, but elsewhere in the galaxy man has gone on to become a relatively civilized animal. *His brain is still the same.* It doesn't change much, because, as I have attempted to point out to you, *man doesn't change that way.* What *did* change, Paul?"

"His culture, of course," Ellery said, feeling a little foolish. "His way of life."

"*Very* good, Paul. Applause. His brain stayed the same—but it had more to work with as man learned more and more. Now, does man inherit his culture?"

"No. It's historically produced. He learns it." Ellery felt like a singularly dull freshman.

"Fine. Very good. You people are bugs on supermen. It's a very common primitive trait. Have another drink."

Ellery had another.

John put his feet back up on the chair and peered at

Ellery intently. "You should think more about man, Paul. Plain old everyday man. He's a remarkable animal."

Ellery waited for John to go on, but John just looked at him, smiling.

"You didn't bring me here tonight just for the hell of it," Ellery said. "I don't know just what your part in all this is, John, but I know there's something that you want me to do. There isn't much time left. You've been talking——"

"That's right," the little fat man said. "I've been doing all the talking, haven't I? And I have accomplished two purposes. The first was to take your mind off yourself. The second was to give you the solution to your problem."

Paul Ellery stared at him, his pipe forgotten in his hand.

19

CHRISTMAS EVE HAD long since turned into Christmas.

The vast bulk of the spaceship floated high in the darkness above the sleeping Earth. It was a shadow, undetected and unseen, slipping through the shifting air currents as a mighty fish might balance itself in a shadowed sea. It moved without sound, wrapped in an envelope of force, proud and aloof over the dark villages it had seeded from the stars.

Alone in one tiny crevice within the leviathan that could swim to the shores of the galaxy, the two men talked.

The talk went on—seemingly trival in a universe vast beyond understanding, just as the Earth was a trivial thing in a galaxy that had passed her by.

But trivia was slippery stuff to define.

Trivia had an unpleasant habit of turning into something else. Trivia was all art and literature and music and love and science, while all sensible people knew that it was battles and wars and headlines that were really important.

All trivia did was to build civilizations.

Sometimes, though, it seemed a little slow. To Ellery, it

didn't seem to be moving at all. "Look here John," he said, "this is one devil of a time to be playing games."

The fat man shrugged. "Depends on what game you're playing," he said.

Ellery helped himself to more Scotch. He was keyed up and tired at the same time, and he had reached that early-morning stage in which a few drinks one way or the other didn't make much difference.

"Let's just pretend that I am a small and rather dull child," he said. "You bring me up here when I have only a few days left before going though a mental meat-grinder, and you tell me why supermen strike you as illogical. You're a good talker, John, and I like to listen to you. But then you tell me that you've just solved my problem for me. Now, unless I'm greatly mistaken, my problem is a simple one. I've got to decide in six days whether or not I'm going to the Center. If I do, I start a new life, with new values. If I don't, I go back to live a life that has become meaningless for me. I can't live like that. You yourself told me, not so very long ago, what I should do. You said: 'If you can't beat 'em, join 'em.' If you've solved that problem, you're going to have to spell it out for me. I haven't got time for riddles."

John frowned, as though disappointed. "I had hopes for you, Paul, or I wouldn't have bothered with all this. I *still* have hopes for you. Let me draw you a small parallel, to help you understand my position. You have been a teacher yourself—I don't know whether you were good, bad, or indifferent, but I suspect that you were indifferent. But let's talk about a *good* teacher. If he's got a student who he thinks has some brains, he can give that student some facts to chew on. He can point out lines of inquiry that may bear fruit. But he can't do *all* the work. The student has got to relate the facts for himself, or else they will never mean anything to him.

Most students never do forge a coherent whole out of the information that gets stuffed into them. Sometimes that's the teacher's fault, Paul. And sometimes it's the student's."

"Okay, okay," Ellery said impatiently. "So where are the facts?"

John sighed.

The aborigines are slow, Ellery thought. *You have to lead them step by step.*

"Let's do a little spelling-out then," John said. "We'll start with fundamentals. I am a man." He waved his hand. "No, I'm not making fun of you. You go ahead and get irritated if you wish, but don't let it keep you from thinking a little."

"Sorry," said Ellery. He refilled his pipe and lit it.

John said, "Very well. I am a man. As a man, I was by chance born into the culture in which you find me, and into a society with its customs and laws and policies. As a man, I have a job to do—I am employed, if you wish. Since I have a certain knack for getting along with natives, I am used by my government in contact work when such is needed. In my official capacity, I first met you. I gave you the business, and I flatter myself that I did it rather well. Now, however, I am not in my official capacity. Now I am trying to talk to you as a man."

"I see," said Ellery. "But can't you be more explicit? If you overestimate my abilities, we won't get very far."

John smiled. "If I have overestimated your abilities," he said, "then you are of no use one way or the other."

Ellery absorbed that. He was getting a bit tired of being patronized, but he knew that John was not doing it without a purpose. There were some people you had to sting into giving the best that was in them.

"I'll tell you why I can't be more explicit," John said. "To put it in a convenient nutshell, I am a law-abiding citizen. I *have* to be. I have not the slightest intention of trying to overthrow my government, and couldn't do it if I wanted to."

Ellery waited, almost hopelessly. If he was going to get anything useful, it would have to be soon. *Very* soon.

John drummed his fingers on his desk. "I'm not much of an idealist, son," he said. "My life has not left me starry-eyed and panting about the fate of the downtrodden. I'm not a reformer. I like to think that I'm a practical man, just as you are."

"What do you mean by practical?"

John brightened visibly. "Ah, semantics! A brain cell has stirred into reluctant life!"

"Dammit, John, climb off your high horse." Ellery smiled. "How would you like a swat on the kisser?"

John laughed, delighted. "Wouldn't bother me in the slightest," he assured him. "And it certainly wouldn't help *you*. But I like your attitude. It's a great improvement. Dish it out a little, Paul. You don't progress by just taking it."

"I'll send your sentiments to Edgar Guest."

John suddenly slammed his fist down with a bang on his desk. He stood up, and Ellery changed his mind in a hurry about what a pushover John might be in a fight.

"Practical!" he snorted. "I'll tell you what's practical. It's just one damned thing: being smart enough to survive. Not just you and me—we're nothing. But all of us, everybody! If man survives he's been practical. If he doesn't, he goes down the drain. What do you think of that?"

"Sounds good. What does it mean, specifically?"

"It means, my friend, that the civilization which I have the honor to represent is typical of man in every way. It's a pack of howling jackasses galloping over a cliff! We've made a lot of so-called progress. We've got spaceships and planets and gadgets a million years ahead of anything on that speck of dirt under our feet. And so what, Paul? I repeat: *so what?*"

Ellery smoked his pipe. Invisibly, he crossed his fingers.

John sat down again and folded his hands patiently. "You already have all the facts you need," he said. "You're supposed to be a scientist. Let me ask you a question. What is the one sure thing about colonial policies, in the long run? The one thing you can always count on?"

Paul Ellery said slowly: "They don't work."

"Fine!" John banged his fist down again and helped himself to most of what was left of the Scotch. "You see before you a civilization that covers the galaxy. You see technological triumphs that you can barely understand. And what are you caught up in the big fat middle of, son? A colony! A backward planet taken over as a colony! You see nothing fantastic about that, Paul? Eh? You see nothing fantastic?"

"I guess I've been a little stupid," Ellery said. His brain was churning, trying to digest what it had swallowed.

"Of course you've been stupid! You're a man, aren't you? What other animal could make the same mistake a billion times and still be around to talk about it?"

"You said," Ellery reminded him carefully, "that you were a law-abiding citizen."

"You bet I am. Most human beings are. That doesn't mean that I have to *agree* with all the laws I live under. If everybody had always agreed that current ideas were the ultimate in human wisdom, we would all still be huddled in caves. Indeed, son, we never would have *reached* the caves! Still, as I have pointed out before, I am a non-political person." He smiled. "Practically."

"And now—what?"

"Now," John told him, "I'm going to show you something. I have, in my small way, tried to set you to thinking about the Others. I hope that the problem has interested you?"

"Of course. What are they?"

"That," said John, "is what I'm going to show you."

The tireless little man surged up from behind his messy desk and led the way across the room, like a halfback leading the interference. Paul Ellery followed in his wake, and hoped he could find out where the ball was.

They passed through the sliding door into the corridor, and John set a fast pace through the ship. They passed a number of men and women, none of whom paid much attention to them. The ship was lighted normally; there seemed to be no difference between night and day on it. Or perhaps they hadn't bothered to adjust themselves to the daily cycle of Earth.

They hustled down long, antiseptic passageways, past a confusing multiplicity of doors, panels, and branching tunnels. They rode on elevators and walked up ramps. Finally, when Ellery judged that they were very high in the floating ship—he almost expected the air to be thinner—they came to a stop before a large, closed door.

There was a guard here—the first one that Ellery had noticed anywhere on the ship. The guard nodded to John, but looked a question at Ellery.

"He's with me," John said. "Everything's all right."

The guard said something, not in English, and activated the door. It slid open noiselessly and John led Ellery inside. Behind them, the door closed again.

The room was not large, and looked almost like a standard projection room. There were some twenty rows of comfortable seats, all of which faced one end of the room. At that end, replacing the standard white screen that would have been found on Earth, was a square of cloudy gray. The square was not just a surface, but was rather an area of well-defined substance, like thick, tinted air, gently in motion.

The two men sat down in the front row. John pressed a combination of buttons in the arm of his chair.

"Meet the Others," he said.

All the lights went out.

The gray square turned a milky white and seemed to fill the room.

Involuntarily, Ellery narrowed his eyes to slits against the smokelike stuff, but there was no sensation.

The milky white shifted into a sharp gray-black. Quite suddenly, Ellery caught his breath and felt a distinct sensation of falling. He held on tightly to the arms of his chair, but the chair was falling too. He tried to breathe and there was no air. There was only a vast black tunnel, bigger than the world, and he was falling down it, head first, toward a billion flashlights that picked him out and blinded him as he fell——

Faster and faster——

He saw three sleek spaceships swimming ahead of him. His eyes fastened on them, desperately. Perspective returned. He could breathe.

The spaceships looked like gray minnows, lost in immensity. They edged along the jet black tunnel, toward the staring flashlights that were a huge spray of stars.

The tunnel widened and became deep space itself. The lights flowed together and made an eye-searing splash of frozen flame. Around the edges, there was a scattering of lesser stars.

This was not the galaxy that had given birth to man.

The three ships slipped on through the clinging ink, with tiny white spots of atomic fire bubbling from their tails. Their movement was lost against the Gargantuan scale, but the splash and drops of light came closer.

There was something else.

Ellery could not quite see it. But he hunched back against his chair, and he wished that he could close his eyes.

He almost saw it. He wanted to scream. He remembered that night, a million years ago, that night in the pale blue lights. . . .

It was naked in space. Unprotected. Alone.

It oozed and undulated in an oily slime.

It came toward the ships and it had eyes.

It did nothing that Ellery could follow, but one of the ships broke in two. Flame licked out into space and dripped. away in every direction. Ellery tried not to see.

The two remaining ships started to turn, curving around in a long, agonizing arc. They were tragically slow. It took them forever——

A pale force started to surround the ships. It grew, shimmering. The ships turned——

And then there was one ship. The other disappeared.

The thing with the eyes *flapped*—that was the only word for it. It hung in empty space, coated with slime. It waited.

The last ship got away. It started back up the long black tunnel, away from the splash of light and the thing that rested in nothing. It blurred, and dimensions changed——

There was milky whiteness again, and then just a square of cloudy gray.

Paul Ellery was back in the projection room.

"Cute, hey?" said John.

Ellery didn't say anything.

The little fat man led the way out of the room and back down the tunnels and ramps and elevators to his office. He poured two glasses of Scotch from a fresh bottle, and this time both men downed them with one long, shuddering drink. John poured two more and sat down.

"That area is known to your astronomers as the Large Magellanic Cloud," John said slowly. "It is an irregular extragalactic star system. It's where the Others live."

"They live in space? Empty space?"

John shrugged. "They're versatile," he said.

"How much do you know about them?"

"Not too much, but enough. There are other galaxies than this one, Paul, and other life-forms than man. The Others are hostile, if that is the right word. Who could possibly understand their motives, if they have any? They have been sighted within our own galaxy, and they mean trouble. Not now, as far as we can tell, but eventually. One day man will have to face them, Paul. If it came today, man would lose. He wouldn't even be in the fight."

Ellery sat very still. His mind seemed suddenly a tiny, hopelessly inadequate thing. His horizons had been blasted open to include a galaxy, and he had tried to face that problem. And now there were other galaxies——

An ant, lost in the jungle.

"It's getting late now," John said, "and the ship will be moving on. Our time is running out on us, Paul, and I may never see you again. I've almost finished what I had to say to you, and maybe it's been something of a disappointment." He waved at the crumpled magazine on his desk. "I flatter myself that I understand you pretty well. You were looking for a secret weapon of some sort, weren't you? A nice miracle, all wrapped up with a blue ribbon?"

Ellery considered. "I tried to tell myself that there wasn't any secret weapon," he said. "But I guess I was looking for one anyway."

John nodded. "There's only one secret weapon that's worth a damn in the long run, Paul. It's the only one you can't beat by dreaming up a better secret weapon. It's called man."

There it is. Your secret weapon.

"You see," said John, talking slowly and clearly now, with none of the exaggerations that Ellery had come to expect, "you've got to get to know us. You must not think of us as a culture—we're human too, Paul. Culture is an abstraction made up from the lifeways of many different people, all averaged together to get the human element out. A galaxy is a large place, and there are many opinions in it. Sentiment among our people, as among all peoples, is divided. We do the best we can. It's the *situation* that breeds the trouble. Hell, my friend, all of us have a long way to go. No system lasts forever. Someday, all men must stand together, or there will be no men left. You've seen the Others now, and I don't think you'll forget them. Just the same, your problem right now is not wandering around out in space somewhere. Your problem is a gent named Paul Ellery. You should get to know him. I think he's a pretty good Joe."

The silence flowed in and filled the air.

Ellery saw the room around him with a curious, sudden clarity. He saw the books, each one distinct in a brightly etched jacket of color. He saw the tapes, gleaming dully. He saw the desk, the chairs, the comforting walls. He saw the bottle, and the stale, filmy glasses. He saw John, and the words that he wanted to say wouldn't come.

"I guess we're not used to friendship these days," he said

slowly. "It embarrasses us. It makes us uncomfortable. We don't know what to do with it."

"I know," John said. "The hell with it, though. If it's there, that's enough."

"Maybe I'll see you again."

"Maybe." John glanced at a clock on his desk. "It's time for you to go."

Ellery stood up, a little shakily. John began to fidget with papers on his desk. Without his solid wall of personality he seemed almost at a loss.

The two men shook hands.

"Hell, boy," John said. "I'll see you around."

"Yeah. Maybe we'll buzz up to heaven and play the same harp."

"Good deal. You'd better roll, Paul, before this crate winds up over Australia somewhere."

"Okay. I know the way. Thanks for everything."

"So long."

Paul Ellery walked toward the door. The door opened.

Behind him, he heard John's voice: "Merry Christmas, son."

The door closed.

He walked down the long passageway, to the globe that would carry him back to Earth. Back to Earth, and back to Jefferson Springs He looked at his watch.

It was almost noon of Christmas Day.

20

THE DAYS THAT were left to Paul Ellery ticked quickly by.
One, two, three——

Four, five, six——

It seemed only a heartbeat, and then it was late morning
on the last day of December. At midnight it would be a new
year on Earth. At one in the morning, the Center ship would
leave for deep space.

There was a place for him on that ship.

All he had to do was climb on board. All he had to do
was kiss the Earth good-by.

He looked outside from his kitchen window. It was a gray,
miserable day. The sun was pale and far away. A cold, biting
wind scratched at the old glass in the window.

Kiss the Earth good-by.

Would that be so tough, really? Sure, it was always hard
to overcome your own inertia, pull up stakes and leave. It was
always hard, but it wouldn't be impossible.

Not now.

There was the diseased, hideous bloom of the hydrogen
flower, waiting to flash into sudden growth on every hillside.

186

There were other charming new flora too—the gray-leafed cobalt tree, and the peaceful nerve-gas-weed.

Ellery had seen war, and seen it close. He had been born in a century of war. He had lived with war always on the horizon. The stink of war was in his nostrils.

Hiroshima and Nagasaki had ushered in a whole new technology. They had made warfare obsolete, and the hydrogen-torn holes in the poorly named Pacific had underlined the lesson. The culture of Earth *had* to change, and would change, but would it change in time?

He had heard the voices so often: "*I say bomb the bastards now while we've got a chance. Hit them before they hit us. Maybe we'll get wiped off the map, but let's take them with us.*"

War was not practical. War was suicide. But people did not know. They reacted as they had always reacted. No one had told them that times had changed. No one had told them that the solutions of twenty years ago were not the solutions of today.

No one had told them.

"*Okay, pal, you tell me a better way.*"

What was there to tell them?

They didn't trust the United Nations.

They could not believe in faith.

They had learned to be cynical in a tough school.

They did not know what science was. They did not know that science was a method. They thought that science was gadgets and bombs and automobiles and television. Why not? The scientists hadn't bothered.

And the scientists were human, too. They weren't just scientists. They were Frank and Sam and Bob and Heinrich and Luigi. They never agreed on anything. It was a point of honor. They would be debating value judgments when the world went *bang*.

There were the men and the women and the children. Each had his problems, his dreams, his fears. Each was right as he saw it. Each was hurrying, trying, working——

Ants in an anthill.

And then the bucket of scalding water.

Ellery wasn't scared of the Preventers. The Galactic Administration could handle them. He wasn't too worried about the Others, not yet. They were a long way from Earth.

Even Jefferson Springs didn't scare him, not by itself.

He wasn't scared of the Americans or the Russians or the Chinese or the English or the Eskimos.

He was afraid of *all* the people.

He was afraid of Earth.

He ground his cigarette out in a dish on the kitchen table and lit another one. He listened to the icebox humming. He heard water dripping from a faucet over the sink. He got up and punched open a can of beer. Outside the window, the world looked very cold.

So much for Earth.

Suppose he left on the alien ship?

First of all, he would live. That was important to him; he could not pretend he wanted to be a martyr. The civilized people of the galaxy had learned to control their bombs. There was no danger of that kind.

If he went to the Center, he would be different. He would not be the same Paul Ellery. Was that any great loss? Was he so crazy about himself that he could not bear any change in great, big, wonderful Paul?

Different, but not completely so. Maybe he would be changed for the better. Certainly, he would be happy. The

Center would see to that. They would give him new values and new goals, and they would equip him to get where he wanted to get.

Wherever that might be.

He would have most of his questions answered—at least the scientific ones. Possibly he could even continue to be an anthropologist, or whatever passed in their culture for an anthropologist. Take the problem of acculturation, for example. Culture change that took place when different cultures came into contact was fascinating stuff. On Earth, scientists were just beginning to get an inkling into the actual nature of the process. At the Center, he could check out a book and get the answers.

The answers to the questions he asked as a man might be more difficult.

He could carve out a life for himself there. A new life, a better life. He could not even imagine the things he might see, the things he might do. He could walk through the future with a notebook. The aliens were people too. He could start over, and face his new life with confidence. He could live in peace, and in safety. He could enjoy himself.

Perhaps, too, he would have an opportunity to help Earth—help her from *inside* the galactic organization. Surely he could do more good there.

Of course, he wouldn't be quite the same, and he might not want to help, and he would be fenced in with laws. But he could still do a lot for Earth. He could be like John.

He tried to believe it.

He looked at his watch. Six o'clock of New Year's Eve. At eight he would be going to Cynthia's to usher in the new year. In seven hours the ship would leave for the Center. He could be on it.

Outside, night had come. He wondered where John was now. He could almost see him here in the kitchen, leaning against the icebox, a glass in his hand. Eyes twinkling, bald pink dome gleaming under the bulb in the ceiling, waving his arms, talking, talking, talking.

John had given him a solution. It was not all tied up in a neat package, but it was there.

The Osage Indians had found oil on their reservation. The oil had been important because it had given them what they needed to amount to something in a commercial culture: money.

John had given him a different kind of oil to deal with a different kind of culture. John had given him information.

Information to bridge the gap.

"It's the *situation* that breeds the trouble," John had said.

The problem posed by the alien colony of Jefferson Springs had no solution because Earth was not far enough advanced to deal with the problem. A problem could not be solved until its existence could be recognized.

"No system lasts forever," John had said.

That was the key. The problem had no solution *at the present time*. That didn't mean that it would *never* have an answer.

The aliens could not legally interfere with Earth, and they enforced their laws. If man could pull himself up the ladder, then the aliens couldn't kick him back down again.

If the Earth could get that far—if there really *was* an Earth and not a patchwork of hostile nations—then the situation would be different. Earth would have found its voice. The alien problem would be understandable, and techniques would have evolved to handle it.

There was more than that. The galactic civilization

would *need* a united Earth by then, and need her desperately. The shoe would be on the other foot. Ellery remembered:

"*Meet the Others.*"

"*If it came today, man would lose.*"

The human galactic civilization was not alone in the universe. Already, it had contacted hostile life-forms from another galaxy, the Others who had no name. Men had discovered that the Others were deadly, and one day they would have to be faced. Perhaps by then they would not have to be met with naked force, but man would still have to be united and strong to survive. There were wheels within wheels, always.

Even the Galactic Administration was young. Beyond the Others, who knew what lay in wait for man? He would need his strength.

Ellery could not deal with the colony now. He could not negotiate because Earth had nothing to offer. Applying the right force at the wrong time was worse than applying no force at all. But the right force at the *right* time—that would work. That would always work. The galactic civilization, too, would be interested in survival.

The solution was there. It was centuries away, but it was there.

In the last analysis, Earth's future was up to Earth. It couldn't wish the responsibility off on anyone else. It could pull itself up by its bootstraps until it was a world to reckon with, or it could blast itself to oblivion. At best, the answer was hundreds of years in the future.

Earth might never get there.

Meanwhile, Paul Ellery had a life to live. He looked at his watch. Eight o'clock. He was late. He still had a decision to make, and there was no use kidding himself. There would be no second chance.

There wasn't much time. The old year was almost gone.

He heard the click of a woman's heels come up the wooden steps to his porch. Cynthia would be doing a slow burn. He walked quickly across the living room and opened the door.

A woman stood there. Not Cynthia.

Anne.

21

HE LOOKED AROUND for some words and couldn't find any.

"Hello, Ell. May I come in, or are the vampires feeding tonight?"

Anne just looked at him, waiting. Her soft gray-green eyes were shadowed and her dark hair was combed a little too hastily. She had on a blue suit with a white blouse, and the skirt was wrinkled from sitting too long.

"Come on in, Annie," Ellery said. "It's cold out there."

She came in, looked around, smiled faintly at the picture that still hung turned toward the wall. She took off her blue suit jacket, fluffed out her hair, and eyed him uncertainly.

"How did you get here?" Ellery asked inanely.

"I took the bus. The public transportation system is still in operation. I'm happy to report. There weren't many passengers tonight."

"Did you have a good trip?"

"Utterly delightful. I knitted you a ski-suit."

"Sorry, Annie. I'm all fouled up tonight. Want some coffee?"

"Not now. Thanks."

She stood there in his living room, looking for some answers of her own. He wanted to go to her but he did not move.

"Annie, why did you come here?"

"I had to come, Paul. I had to see for myself. We've always spent our New Year's Eves together—I didn't think you could forget them. I wanted to see her, whoever she is. I guess I just couldn't stand it." Her voice was less steady now. "I'm *not* going to cry."

"You shouldn't have come."

"I know that. I'm here, though." She managed a smile. "What are you going to do with me?"

"I'm going to ask you a favor, hon," he said slowly. "Will you do me one more favor?"

"I'll try, Ell. What shall I do—go out to the crossroads and drive a stake through her heart?"

"It's tougher than that. I've got to go out. I want you to wait here and not follow me. I'll leave you my car, just in case."

She looked at him, desperately. "What *is* all this, Paul? Are you in some kind of trouble?"

"You might put it that way," Ellery said. "Look, I can't answer your questions. I just can't. You'll have to trust me. I want you to wait here. Will you do that, hon?"

She nodded, not understanding. "How long do I wait, Paul?"

"Wait until one," he said. "I know I'm asking a lot—I would have saved you from this if I could. I tried. If I'm not back by one, take my car and go home and forget me."

"I guess I asked for it, Ell."

"I've got to go."

She was in his arms. He held her tightly, afraid to let her go. He tore himself away.

He grabbed a coat and left.

The night was raw and cold. A chill wind out of the north sighed through the flat streets and whistled nakedly through the bare branches of the trees.

He had less than four hours left.

He walked through the dark streets of the town. The rows of little boxlike houses squatted along the sidewalks, staring at him. Once he saw a glimmer of pale blue light leaking through a crack in a window. His footsteps clicked on the sidewalk. They made a lonely, hollow sound.

Jefferson Springs seemed utterly deserted around him.

He climbed the steps of Cynthia's house and knocked on the door. He walked inside without waiting to be asked.

"Well," said Cynthia, getting to her feet from the couch, "fancy meeting you here."

"Sorry I'm late."

"Sober?"

"Yes."

"This is your big night, lover. Want a drink?"

"Sure."

Cynthia poured him one of her inspired dry Martinis, which he insulted by drinking it at a gulp. She made him another, and kissed him.

"Relax, baby," she said. "Don't you want to get civilized?"

He sat down on the couch. She looked terrific. She always did. Her blond hair was smooth as silk, her blue eyes cool as ice. Her dress was wicked. Cynthia knew how to use clothes.

"I've been lonesome. I'll miss you, Paul."

"Sure you will."

"What's eating you, lover?"

"Cannibals." He laughed, unreasonably.

"You're nervous. I'll fix you another one."

The Martinis warmed him. He could not think. He postponed his thinking and tried to relish what he had come here to do.

Quite suddenly it was eleven o'clock. Time was running out.

"Cyn."

"Yes?"

"I came here to tell you something."

"Say it, then."

The room pressed in around them. A warm room, secure against the outside cold.

He stood up. "I came here to say a lot of things, Cyn. I wanted to call you a bitch and tell you all about yourself. I wanted to tell you I knew what you were after—you wanted to sleep with a caveman, try out one of the natives for kicks. I've known it ever since the dance, maybe before. That's all I was to you, just a savage to play with. I wanted to tell you that I knew all about that. I wanted to say I stayed with you because you were the best I could get. I had it all planned. I was going to walk in here and toss it in your teeth and see how you liked it. It's funny as hell, Cyn. I've been nursing this for a long time—and now it doesn't seem worth doing. So where do we go from here?"

Cynthia sipped her Martini calmly. "I knew you knew, Paul."

He sat down, feeling hollow.

She lit a cigarette. "Baby, we are what we are. Maybe

you're just beginning to find that out. I'm a misfit here and so are you. I was lonely, too, if you like. I was *bored*. That was my crime. These people of mine are the supreme bores of all creation, if you want my honest opinion. They're here because they didn't have enough on the ball to stay home. I'm here because I didn't fit in any place. I'm just not a solid citizen, lover. I was alone, and you were something new. You were alone, so I gave myself to you. We had fun, didn't we, Paul? Does that make me evil? Does that make me a bitch?"

"Score one for your team," Ellery said.

She shrugged. "I'll go my way, Paul. I always have. When it's all over I'll have no regrets. When you get back from the Center, if they send you here, come on around and say hello."

"I won't be very interesting then. No more caveman."

She smiled, "We'll see."

"I've got to go, Cyn. Thanks for everything."

"Good luck, lover."

She kissed him, and then he was outside. He put on his coat, shivering in the cold, and looked at his watch.

Midnight. The time was now.

A metallic globe from the Center ship was waiting for him on the Walls Ranch. He would have to get outside the city limits and then pass the Garvin Berry place. Jim Walls lived in the next house. It was not too far to walk. It might take him half an hour—no more than that.

He stood in the cold wind, fists clenched, eyes closed. He had waited. Waited until the last possible minute. He was caught now. He was forced into it. He had to move one way or the other.

He watched to see what he would do.

The ship was waiting, half an hour away. Peace was

waiting, a short walk down the road. A new life was waiting,
waiting in a metal sphere.

He had his chance.

He smiled. He started to walk.

His steps clicked on the cold cement. Jefferson Springs
was dark and cold around him. He walked through a village
of the dead.

He did not walk alone. Memories of Earth walked with
him.

Austin. A hot summer day. The lake around the alumi-
num canoe, still and glassy calm. The sun on his bare
shoulders. Hank and Chuck drinking warm beer and munch-
ing stale bread. The fish that wouldn't bite. The wonderful,
sharp coolness of the water when they had tossed aside the
bamboo poles and lowered themselves into the green, green
lake. . . .

Home. A living room filled with the very special lamps
and pictures and chairs that had been his world. Mom humming over the dishes in the kitchen. Dad laughing at some
book he was reading. "Pop, can I have a dime for a soda? All
the guys are going. Can I Pop?" His street outside, and the
dark sunset trees. . . .

Los Angeles. A party late at night after a convention.
Stale smoke in the air. George and Lois Sage sitting across
from him. Everyone talking about what to do if an air-raid
alert sounded. Everyone scared of the hydrogen bomb. Lois
smiling. "Personally, I'm going to catch a bus for downtown
L.A. That way you get vaporized all at once and miss the
painful flash-burns. . . .

Colorado. A tiny village nestled at the foot of a pass
through the snow-capped mountains. Blue sky, clean air, tall
pines. A swift river filled with trout. An unshaven old man

with his shirttail out. "Sonny, I remember this town when the mines was here and they brung in a hundred whores from Denver. . . ."

New York. Bright lights. A little club, a hole in the wall. A Dixieland band. A trumpeter almost completely paralyzed, playing in a wheelchair. Pale face sweating under the white lights. *Aunt Hagar's Blues.* A flushed, excited grin. "You had it then, Johnny, you had it then. . . ."

God, it was funny—the things you remembered.

You never knew how much they meant to you.

He walked faster. Down one street, across another. The cold forgotten now.

Hurry, hurry, don't be late——

Don't be late for your new world. Don't be late for your new life!

He had found his place. He had found his people. The odds against him in the only life he could ever know were tremendous. He was a fool——

He didn't give a damn.

Hurry, hurry, don't be late——

Earth had a chance. He had only to believe in it. He had to have only a little faith, a little hope.

Earth was his.

He had a job to do. A little job, a job that paved the way. It was not the business of science to dictate to others. It was not the business of science to force people to its ways. All it could do was make the facts available to all, honestly and without fear.

Science, too, had to have faith in man.

Hurry, hurry, don't be late——

No man could say what might make the difference between chaos and civilization.

It might be a word in a classroom.

It might be one more man who would stand up and be counted.

It might be a faked community study to make men think a little.

There was the high school, frozen under the stars.

He began to run.

Across the street, past his parked car, up the steps of his house. He jerked open the door, ran inside.

And stopped.

Anne wasn't there. But——

He saw her then. In the kitchen, drinking coffee. She looked up, startled.

"Paul!"

He kissed her. He kissed her neck and her eyes and her hair. He knocked over the coffee pot. The hell with it!

"Happy New Year, Annie," he whispered. "Happy New Year!"

"Paul!"

"Quick now, Annie! Grab everything of mine you can get your hands on. Throw it in the car. Hurry!"

"But——"

"Are you too proud to marry me, Annie?"

Her mouth made a big round O. She looked at him speechlessly and then pitched in with the energy of a demon. They cleaned the house out in nothing flat. They turned out all the lights and piled into the Ford.

They laughed at nothing, at everything.

He gunned the engine and the tires screeched as he pulled away from the curb. He drove down the street as fast as he dared to drive. Right on Main Street. Past the shadowed square of the ice-house.

Out onto the open road.

Hurry, hurry, don't be late—

Past the Berry place. Past Jim Wall's ranch. The gray sphere was out there in the field, waiting for him. He could feel the prodigious might that hung high above his head, blotting out the stars.

He did not look up. He looked straight ahead.

"If you can't beat 'em, join 'em!"

That had more than one meaning. If you can't beat 'em the way they are now, then catch up with them!

"Hang on, Annie," he grinned. "Here we go!"

They went the back way, across the beautiful and lonely land. Up to Uvalde, over to Kerrville, on through the Hill Country.

There were stars all around them.

Far ahead in the east, where the low, dark hills touched the sky, Ellery could see the first faint rays from the morning sun. Beneath the rising sun, his city waited.

He prayed that this warm, golden sun might be the only one his home would ever know. He prayed that another manmade sun might never sear its shadows across his Earth.

He laughed, exultantly, into the night.

It was good to fight for life.

John was very near and smiling.

Anne was close at his side.

"Paul, it's so good to have you back!"

"It's good to be back," he said. "Annie, Annie, you'll never know how wonderful it is to be back."

THERE ARE CERTAIN predictable questions that a writer is asked, and they appear with awesome regularity. When did you start writing? (Exactly twenty minutes after the invention of movable type.) Where do you get your ideas? (In New Jersey, usually.) Do you write at specific times? (Yes. No matter when I write, the time is never ambiguous.) What is your best book? (I have a collection of Shakespeare's plays that I think shows a great deal of talent.) What name do you write under? (Hemingway. It has a kind of a ring to it, and therefore I have printed it on the ceiling over my desk.)

One question that I have never been asked is this one: Of all the stories you have written, which one is closest to your heart? The answer to that question is *Shadows in the Sun*.

I have been told, by those learned souls who are supposed to know about such things, that nobody pays much attention to comments by an author. They are just there, like parsley on a plate. I don't know. Personally, I have a sneaking fondness for prefaces and introductions and postscripts. They are brief visits with friends I know or would like to know. I always read them first, whether or not I ever get around to reading the books they decorate.

It may be that you are a kindred spirit. It is even possible that you might be interested in knowing why *Shadows in the Sun* has the hold on me that it does. If not, there is a simple remedy available. Just stop reading.

I was only twenty-five when I wrote *Shadows in the Sun*, and that is a good age for a writer to be. I was old enough to have some experience with this odd adventure called life and young enough to believe that all things were possible—even a good novel. I did not know what I could or could not do, and so I went ahead and did them.

Shadows in the Sun is the most autobiographical of my novels, but of course it is not a literal autobiography. I am not (was not) Paul Ellery, although he occasionally comes rather too close for comfort. The only spaceships I saw in the skies over the town I called Jefferson Springs were in my imagination. Aliens? Well, I'll get to them in a moment.

If *Shadows in the Sun* is not autobiography in the conventional sense of the term, it is nevertheless an intensely personal book. I cannot read it without a curious sense of going back in time and encountering myself. So there you are, Chad Oliver. A young primate, frozen in amber. See? This is what you were, and where you were. These are the people you knew. This is what you thought, felt, believed. . . .

Consider: after having lived my early years in Cincinnati, Ohio, where I was born, I moved to a small town in Texas at the end of my sophomore year in high school. Cincinnati was and is a large city, and the Olivers had been there since approximately Paleolithic times. Quite suddenly, I found myself in a little Texas town. Population: 6,000. San Antonio was 120 miles in one direction, and Mexico was 60 miles in the other.

I was not an anthropologist then. I was a teen-aged boy trying to adapt to an environment as strange to me as anything on Mars. Yes, in that sense I was like Paul Ellery. Discovering. Understanding. Often alone. (There was one other transplanted Yankee in the high school. He became my closest friend and remained so until his death a few years ago. When I gave the eulogy at his funeral, those years in "Jefferson Springs" seemed like only yesterday.) And yes, there were aliens in that town, attempting to cope with a new way of life. Jim and I *were* the aliens. Perhaps that is why the aliens in this book are not as monstrous as the aliens who slither through so much of science fiction.

Even then, "Jefferson Springs" was beginning to change. If that were not so, I would not have been there. I do not doubt that by now virtually the entire population *has* been replaced. Certainly, the last time I visited the place I was almost a stranger again. But what I found during the years that I lived there was warmth and acceptance. The people were very good to this alien. I played football, and maybe that had something to do with it. I edited the yearbook. I edited and wrote the school paper. (I had one serial that I used as filler. It involved a confrontation between Sherlock Holmes and Frankenstein, and it baffled the whole town.) My discoveries included females. (Paul Ellery again?) Those were happy years. That is why I tend to be impatient with novels that portray small towns—Texan or otherwise—as outposts of unmitigated barbarism. That is why, I think, that a fair amount of unabashed affection has found its way into *Shadows in the Sun*.

I can hear a faintly querulous voice asking, But what about science fiction? What about anthropology? One might respond, How can there be good science fiction, or good fiction of any kind, that has no contact with reality? One might even ask the same question with regard to anthropology.

We don't have to be that pretentious, however.

I devoured science fiction. I absorbed it before I ever came to Texas. I read it all through high school, surviving polite suspicion as the village lunatic. I continued to read it (how much time we had then!) during my student years at the University of Texas. I was a *part* of it when I was in graduate school at UCLA. I had actually met the gods: Bradbury, Van Vogt, Kuttner, and so many others. I had written a novel, *Mists of Dawn*, and I was writing for *Astounding* and *The Magazine of Fantasy and Science Fiction*. I kept on reading; it is quite possible that I read it all. I do not know how many millions of words of science fiction I had read when I was twenty-five years old. I do know that every word contributed to the writing of *Shadows in the Sun*. This was not a book written by someone who had only a casual interest in the field. Science fiction was a vital part of whatever it was that made me tick. Going back to the novel now, I confess that I remain pleased by the degree to which I avoided many of the sins that plague routine, conventional science fiction. Still, you cannot escape the clichés unless you know what they are—and perhaps even have a certain fondness for them. (You might have some fun with a story called "The Last Word," which I wrote with Charles Beaumont. In that one, we gleefully used them all. You can find it in *The Best From Fantasy and Science Fiction*, 5th Series, edited by Anthony Boucher, and more recently in *Evil Earths*, edited by Brian

Aldiss.) I don't mean to suggest, of course, that *Shadows in the Sun* is a flawless novel, or that I was alone in searching for new directions for science fiction. After all, both Ted Sturgeon's magnificent *More Than Human* and Arthur Clarke's masterpiece, *Childhood's End*, were published while I was completing *Shadows in the Sun*. There was no shortage of competition. I would only say that *Shadows in the Sun* was a labor of love, and that I was trying to build from within rather than to attack from without. I was excited by what I felt science fiction could be and what it could say. I would not be unhappy if you called it a vision. That fire is not out yet, although the flames are a little older now.

I plead guilty to being a man of many enthusiasms. As I have indicated, I was a graduate student at UCLA when I wrote this novel, working on a Ph.D. in anthropology. I was drenched in anthropology, as only a graduate student can be with his or her orals looming on the horizon. I believed in it, and more than that. I felt that the insights of anthropology might well save this world of ours. There is a lot of anthropological thinking built into the very structure of this book, and it is state-of-the-art as of the time it was written. I had one distinguished professor who was kind enough to tell me that he had read *Shadows in the Sun* and made up his mind then and there to award me my degree. He didn't tell me that until after I had my Ph.D., however.

It is somewhat disconcerting to see Paul Ellery turning again and again to his anthropological training, seeking answers that were not there. I am relieved to encounter an occasional cautionary passage, but Paul certainly had the faith. I would not judge him too harshly. Paul was young, and he was supremely innocent of the dark puzzles of university budgets, personality conflicts between scientists, and political editorials disguised as research. I wonder if he would find more answers today. I do not know, but I am convinced that he would find some compelling questions in modern anthropology. My enthusiasms, I fear, are not ephemeral.

I have not changed a word of the text in this edition of *Shadows in the Sun.* It is sometimes hard to resist tinkering, but it seems to me that the novel is very much a product of a particular time and place. I could change it, perhaps for the better, but I have no urge to do so. It is a hopeful book, and conceivably even a statement about the human spirit. Inadequate as it may be, I'll go with that.

I have also left the original dedication intact. I once had a professor, beguiled by Freudian mythology, who assured me that it was flatly impossible to love both your father and your mother. At the very least, it was distinctly unfashionable. Well, my father has been dead now these many years, but never forgotten for a day. My mother is slowly recovering from a massive stroke, and she may not be able to read these words. I will read them to her.

This one is still for you, folks.

—Austin, Texas
April 1985